GODS' GAMES WE PLAY

2

**PEARL**

She jumps to conclusions a bit too quickly but has shown surprising ability as a member of Fay's team.

**FAY**

A game lover whom some call humanity's greatest hope. His team includes Leshea and Pearl.

**DAX**

An elite apostle who carries Mal-ra's hopes on his shoulders. Sees Fay as his rival.

**KELRITCH**

Supports Dax. Insists she isn't interested in him...

"L-Leshea! Those aren't...

Hngh! Those aren't coins!"

**LESHEA**

The former Dragon God Leoleshea. A true game lover who recently awoke from a 3,000-year nap.

"These coins are so soft..."

AT THE OASIS...?

# GODS' GAMES WE PLAY 2

# GODS' GAMES WE PLAY

Kei Sazane

Illustration by Toiro Tomose

YEN ON

New York

# Volume | 2

## Kei Sazane

**Translation by** Kevin Steinbach

**Cover art by** Toiro Tomose

This book is a work of fiction. Names, characters, places, and incidents are the product of the author's imagination or are used fictitiously. Any resemblance to actual events, locales, or persons, living or dead, is coincidental.

KAMI WA GAME NI UETEIRU. Vol.2
©Kei Sazane 2021
First published in Japan in 2021 by KADOKAWA CORPORATION, Tokyo.
English translation rights arranged with KADOKAWA CORPORATION, Tokyo, through TUTTLE-MORI AGENCY, INC., Tokyo.

English translation © 2023 by Yen Press, LLC

First Yen On Edition: June 2023
Edited by Yen On Editorial: Leilah Labossiere
Designed by Yen Press Design: Andy Swist

Yen On is an imprint of Yen Press, LLC.
The Yen On name and logo are trademarks of Yen Press, LLC.

The publisher is not responsible for websites (or their content) that are not owned by the publisher.

Yen On
150 West 30th Street, 19th Floor
New York, NY 10001

Visit us at yenpress.com
facebook.com/yenpress
twitter.com/yenpress
yenpress.tumblr.com
instagram.com/yenpress

Library of Congress Cataloging-in-Publication Data
Names: Sazane, Kei, author. | Tomose, Toiro, illustrator. |
    Steinbach, Kevin, translator.
Title: Gods' games we play / Kei Sazane ; illustration by Toiro Tomose ;
    translation by Kevin Steinbach.
Other titles: Kami ha game ni ueteiru. English
Description: First Yen On edition. | New York, NY : Yen On, 2022-
Identifiers: LCCN 2022033520 | ISBN 9781975348496 (v. 1 ; trade paperback) |
    ISBN 9781975348519 (v. 2 ; trade paperback)
Subjects: CYAC: Fantasy. | Gods—Fiction. | Games—Fiction. |
    Competition (Psychology)—Fiction. | LCGFT: Fantasy fiction. | Light novels.
Classification: LCC PZ7.1.S297 Go 2022 | DDC [Fic]—dc23
LC record available at https://lccn.loc.gov/2022033520

ISBNs: 978-1-9753-4851-9 (paperback)
        978-1-9753-4852-6 (ebook)

10 9 8 7 6 5 4 3 2 1

LSC-C

Printed in the United States of America

# Character

## Fay

People expect great things from this apostle, the best rookie in recent memory. His new team also includes Leshea and Pearl.

## Leshea

Full name Leoleshea. A former god who awoke after three thousand years sleeping in ice. She adores playing games.

## Pearl

An apostle who possesses teleportation abilities. She once earned herself the nickname Assumption-Autopilot Girl, which should tell you how much trouble she can cause.

## Dax

"The Hope of Mal-ra." Sees Fay as his rival, though Fay doesn't know that yet.

## Kelritch

Dax's team member and right-hand woman. Dax may be keen on Fay, but Kelritch sure isn't.

## Nel

A former apostle from Mal-ra, forced to retire by loss count.

# Story

The gods' games: the ultimate game experience, created by all-powerful gods with way too much time on their hands. Anyone who wins ten of these games will be granted an incredible gift, but so far, no one in human history has managed it. That hasn't stopped them from trying, though, and right now their best hope seems to lie with a young man named Fay and a young woman (and former god) named Leshea. Together with another young lady named Pearl, they're the newest team to tackle the gods' games. A team that everyone has heard of since they posted a victory against Uroboros, one of the toughest opponents around. It took every ounce of their wits and skill to triumph, but it means the *whole world* knows about them now...

# Prologue
## The Failure

**Time Elapsed: 57 hours, 8 minutes, 41 seconds**

"Seal of Fire (motto: 'A brand carved in flame'): twenty-one members down."
"Three members remaining."

That was enough to strike despair in the hearts of all who heard it. Our group of young go-getters had thrown ourselves into the gods' games, only to be confronted with an impossibly difficult match. After almost sixty hours of intense battle, our team members were dropping like flies. Now there were only three of us left, including me.

This game, Topple the God, involved literally bringing a god to its knees—and you needed at least four people to do it. Checkmate.

After a very long silence, the apostles to my left and right raised their hands to the heavens and said: "We forfeit."

I gnashed my teeth and howled with every fiber of my being.

\*     \*     \*

"Captain! Vice Captain! Wait! This game isn't over! Three of us are still standing! Please! I don't want it to end this way! It can't end like—"

━━━━━━━━━

"Huh?!" The young woman sat up abruptly and jumped out of bed like a spring, kicking the light blanket she'd been wrapped in toward the ceiling. She stood, breathing hard. It was only as she began to catch her breath in the dim room, lit by the modicum of sun that slipped past the curtains, that she realized it had been a dream. In her sleep, she'd been revisiting her last day as an apostle, when her defeat in one of the gods' games had forced her to retire.

"Again... It keeps coming back to me in my dreams," she mumbled, sweat beading on her forehead. The tank top she slept in was so soaked that it felt heavy. She couldn't believe how much she'd been perspiring.

She uncurled the fingers of her left hand, her palm damp. Three bluish scars in the middle of her hand represented her three losses in the gods' games. The reason she was no longer an apostle. The mark of a failure.

"I still can't get over it... I still can't let it go."

The phone at the head of her bed started ringing.

"Nel! Serious stuff! Take a look at the Arcane Court livestream, quick!"

The voice on the other end belonged to a good friend of hers. "Morning, Anna. What's got you so worked up?"

"It's Ruin! The Sacrament City! Ruin's streaming a game right now!"

Ruin? She remembered that city becoming a topic of global conversation about a year earlier when news had broken of a so-called "god" found deep beneath the ice. Supposedly, this god had been asleep for three millennia. It was an unprecedented discovery.

"So they're streaming a game. They do that all the time," Nel said. She turned on the screen mounted to her wall—and when she saw what it showed, Nel Reckless froze in shock with the phone still in her hand.

*"The gods smile on those who make their own miracles. Right, Uroboros?!"*

The screen showed a young man staring down a titanic black dragon: the Endless God, Uroboros. Uroboros was considered unbeatable, its challenge impossible, yet the boy was facing it head-on.

*"That's the strategy for you, isn't it, Uroboros? Let the god bring down the god."*

The dragon's bellow filled the sky, and the young man on-screen became the first person in history to defeat the Endless God.

There came such cheering from outside that it threatened to shatter the dorm's reinforced glass windows. There must have been tens of thousands of people there in the Sacred Spring City of Mal-ra watching the stream. Nel assumed every city in the world was in an uproar just like this. For that matter, so was she. Her whole body felt hot, as if a flame were igniting in the depths of her heart. There had been such passion, such fervor, in the battle.

"I...I never knew such stirring gameplay existed!" she said. Until the actual moment of victory, the boy had been a hairbreadth from defeat. Yet it had only made his eyes shine even brighter. *As if he was having the time of his life.* As the other apostles had dropped out or been defeated, he'd forged ahead, snatching an unlikely victory from the jaws of disaster.

*I knew it! I knew I was right,* Nel thought. No matter how many teammates you lost, no matter how fearsome the foe was, you couldn't give up. That was what she wished she could have communicated on that fateful day.

"Anna, what's his name? Tell me his name!"

"What? You mean you don't know, Nel? He was all the talk six months back. You know, most amazing rookie this, humanity's greatest hope that?"

"*That's* Fay?!"

So that was the rookie Fay Theo Philus. The one who'd taken five victories in the gods' games in seemingly no time after joining the Arcane Court. It was such an impressive performance that even Arcane Court headquarters was said to have its eye on him.

"Wow..." Nel swallowed. She suddenly discovered her throat was dry. She felt a tension—and an excitement—she'd almost forgotten. "So he's Fay..."

She'd started clenching her fist again without realizing she was doing it. She'd finally found it—she could feel it.

"Anna," she said. "I'm going to work for his team."

"You're going to what?! Nel, are you feeling okay?"

"I'll need to find out what the requirements are for joining him. Once it's all settled, I'll have to move to Ruin. Gotta find a reasonably priced dorm in the Sacrament City."

"Nel, are you listening to me?!"

No. No, she wasn't. Her friend's voice no longer reached Nel's ears. "Master Fay," she said, clutching the phone.

"I, Nel Reckless, vow to offer up my very life to you!"

# Player. 1
## The World Games Tour

# 1

A golden dawn broke over the Sacrament City of Ruin, the sun's rays stretching across the horizon. The local branch of the Arcane Court was sparsely populated, many of its employees not yet on duty. But a few key personnel were there—and at the moment one of them was yelling very, very loudly.

"Mirandaaa! Miranda, I'm talking to you!"

"Ow! O-ouch, that hurts, Leshea! Hrk! The friction of my butt on the floor is going to rub my buns clean off!"

"M...my neck! I can't...breathe...!"

The yells were coming from a certain former god. She stormed down a deserted hallway, dragging a dark-haired young man— Fay—and a golden-haired young woman—Pearl—behind her.

The former god in question was the Dragon God Leoleshea. She appeared to be a young woman with vermilion hair the color of blazing flames. In reality, she was a genuine deity who had descended from the superior spiritual realm, but as she steam-rolled down that hallway, her amber eyes glittered with curiosity and there was a girlish flush in her cheeks.

Fay managed to choke out, "Leshea!" She had him by the collar and was pulling him down the corridor. He was within an inch of suffocating. "You're kinda strangling me, here!"

Pearl started up a lament of her own. "M-my buns are gone and now I'm gonna have a flat bottom foreverrr!" Leshea had the other girl by the collar as well, and she obviously wasn't enjoying her very rounded bottom's long slide across the floor.

"I'm here, Miranda! You'd better be ready!" Leshea cried. There was a grating screech as she wrenched open the locked mechanical door to the chief secretary's office. She made it look as easy as if the door were made of paper.

"And a very good morning to you, Lady Leoleshea," said a woman holding a cup of coffee. She greeted them with a deep, respectful bow. She was Chief Secretary Miranda, the head of this office. As one might expect from a longtime professional, her almond-shaped eyes radiated intelligence. "You might be interested to know that I've been on duty all night and was just thinking about going to bed..."

Leshea completely ignored her. "I held up my end of the bargain!" She pointed to her left, where Pearl was rubbing her behind, tears still welling in her eyes.

"Owww," the blond girl mumbled.

"I accepted Pearl! She's an official member of the team with me and Fay!"

"So I see. And that makes three," Miranda replied. The gods' games were matches of one god against many people, so teams at the Arcane Court had to consist of at least three members.

"Right! I've got the numbers. I've got a proper team. So let me at the gods' games!"

"Sorry, no."

"Why not?!" Leshea cried out as she threw herself over

Miranda's desk. "You're the one who told me that if I got a team together, I could play!"

The chief secretary calmly sipped her decaf coffee. "That's true. However, your team, milady, is only three people—the absolute minimum size. In such cases, we expect multiple teams to dive together so that there are at least ten apostles in any given game."

"Well, then, it's as good as done!" Leshea said. Fay's team might only have three people, but after they'd defeated Uroboros, they'd been deluged with requests from other teams to tackle the gods' games together. "We just round up a couple other teams, make sure we have ten people, and then we can dive right in!"

"I'm afraid you can't."

"Why *not*?!" Leshea wailed again.

Miranda sighed. "Fay, part of your job is to talk Lady Leshea down when she gets like this."

Fay nodded from where he sat on the couch but didn't move. "I stopped her from charging straight into the Dive Center downstairs. But I thought you might do a better job than I could explaining the nuances, Chief Secretary."

Miranda smiled a bit defeatedly. "And that's what brings you here, huh? Very well." She turned on a large wall-mounted screen and started navigating the display. "If you'd be so kind as to have a look at this, Lady Leshea."

"What is it?" Leshea asked.

"The Dive Request status of the Divine Gates in the branch office's possession. We have five in total, although because one of them is currently out of use, only four are available."

Divine Gate I: Teams on waitlist: 13 (Total 241 people). Expected wait time for Dive: 29 days.

Divine Gate II: Teams on waitlist: 17 (Total 277 people). Expected wait time for Dive: 34 days.

Divine Gate III: Teams on waitlist: 14 (Total 201 people). Expected wait time for Dive: 64 days.

Divine Gate IV: Teams on waitlist: 19 (Total 283 people). Expected wait time for Dive: 33 days.

A Divine Gate was, simply defined, a door to another dimension. They were artifacts from the era of the ancient magical civilization—huge stone statues in the shapes of the gods. Pass through the doors of light that emanated from them, and a human could "dive" into Elements, the gods' playground.

"So, ahem, Miranda. How exactly does this work?" Leshea asked.

"*You get in line and wait,*" the chief secretary said, pushing her glasses up the bridge of her nose with a finger. "You know how when you want to go to the most popular ride at the amusement park, you might end up stuck in line for three hours? It's just like that. All functioning Divine Gates are booked well into the future."

"What? But how can that be?!" Leshea said, her eyes wide. They'd been able to dive immediately for the games against Titan and Uroboros.

"I really hate to break it to you, but it's because of you and Fay," Miranda replied with a shrug. "Think about it. You beat Uroboros, right?"

"Yeah, so?"

"You can't imagine how exciting that was to watch. It was a huge victory, something no one in human history had done before. It made a lot of teams want to get out there themselves— and inspired a lot of rivals." The Ruin branch office was home to some one thousand two hundred apostles, and it looked like virtually all of them had requested to dive at once.

"Umm, Chief Secretary?" Pearl had finally massaged her backside enough to sit down on the sofa. "If we put in our dive request right now, how long do you think we'll have to wait?"

"The shortest line is for Divine Gate I—about a month. Past game-time data suggests games could go long, though, in which case you'd naturally have to wait longer than that."

"All right, I get it." Leshea nodded and smiled. "Pearl, we're going. The Dive Center is in the first basement, right?"

"We are? Why are we going?" Pearl said.

"We're going to steal a Divine Gate. By force."

"You can't be serious?!"

The Dragon God Leshea was already practically skipping out of the room. Pearl grabbed her in a hug from behind, desperately trying to hold her back.

"You see what I have to deal with, Chief Secretary Miranda?" Fay gestured to her. "I think this could turn dangerous. No telling what damage Leshea might do if she goes into game withdrawal."

"Hmm..."

"I don't suppose you have any ideas? Something that would allow us to skip the line and get right into the gods' games without screwing over all the other apostles politely waiting their turn?"

"I can think of one thing," Miranda said.

"You can?!" This time it was Fay's turn to shout. For him, it had been an offhand question, a way of trying to get Leshea to give up on the stealing-a-Divine-Gate thing. He'd never expected there might actually be a way.

"I was hoping I wouldn't have to mention this to you or Lady Leshea. Our office was going to just quietly decline." Miranda downed the rest of her coffee in a single gulp. "Eyes back on the monitor, if you don't mind."

The image on-screen changed and the five Divine Gates disappeared to reveal a single email.

### Invitation to the World Games Tour (WGT)

"Uhh, Miranda... What's this?" asked a stunned Leshea. "A...tour?"

"It's like how athletes might be invited to play in tournaments in other countries. From the moment you bested Uroboros, we've been getting messages from all around the world begging to have you go play in their games."

"Why would they do that?"

"I think you might not fully understand what you accomplished. An apostle who takes victory in one of the most brutal of the gods' games is guaranteed to become a global hero. You're a sensation!" Miranda glanced at the monitor with a sort of smile. "The Divine Gates here in Ruin are booked solid, but there may well be other cities where you could dive immediately."

"Well, what are we waiting for? Let's go!"

"Maybe you could at least pretend to hesitate? I am sorry to hear you say that," Miranda said.

"Why?" Leshea asked.

"Because we'd hate to lose you." The chief secretary fiddled with the remote, and the image on the screen changed again.

"Oh, I know this game! That's Fay and Leshea's match against Titan, isn't it?" Pearl said, pointing at the screen. "I watched that. I think everyone in Ruin has probably seen the stream by now!"

"Precisely. The Dragon God Leoleshea and the rookie Fay in a battle for the ages—it drove our viewership through the roof. Even Arcane Court headquarters was watching. *Which is why* this is a problem." Miranda heaved a sigh. "You guys pull in viewers like nothing else, which makes you a very valuable part of the office's income stream. If you go to another city, all that money dries up."

Fay, Leshea, and Pearl currently worked at the Ruin branch office of the Arcane Court, but that didn't stop other cities from trying to tempt this very profitable trio to a new location. Hence the WGT.

"I get it. That can't be a lot of fun for you, Chief Secretary Miranda," Fay said.

"I assure you, Fay, it's not. That's why I intended to turn them down on your behalf. But with Lady Leshea so insistent…"

Leshea didn't want to waste another minute—she wanted to play in the gods' games. For that, she needed a Divine Gate to dive through. But Ruin's gates were all spoken for. Finding an available gate in another city was her only option.

*That wouldn't be great for morale here at the Ruin office, though*, Fay thought. *Knowing someone had poached their most popular team.* The various branch offices of the Arcane Court were all in the same business of trying to conquer the gods' games, but they were also rivals.

"I can see that there's no way out of this," Miranda said, sighing the biggest sigh in history and crossing her arms. "I'll let the WGT know that you accept, Lady Leshea. I'm sure that when you arrive at whatever far-flung branch office, they'll have a Divine Gate available so you can dive right away."

"You will?! They will?! Yippee!"

"Your joy is our office's sorrow. But in any event… Pearl, put out your hands, would you? Palms up."

"Er… Like this?" Pearl said, holding out her hands. There was a mark on each palm, sort of like a tattoo. One was red, the other blue. On her right hand, the roman numeral II was inscribed in crimson. Her left bore a numeral I in azure. These were the marks of the gods. They revealed a person's record in the gods' games. Pearl had two wins and one loss, hence the II on her right hand and the I on her left.

"Wow! Look, Fay! I've got the number II on my right hand, too!" Leshea exclaimed, her eyes shining with curiosity. "Huh? But why isn't there anything on my left hand?"

"'Cause you've never lost a game, Leshea. Same as me." Fay bore a V on his right hand but nothing on his left. In other words, he was five and oh against the gods.

"Stunning," Miranda remarked with a glance at his hand. "Especially you, Fay." She almost sounded irritated by it. "Five is a number you'll see around. Most branch offices have maybe one, maybe two apostles who have reached that level. Doing it with zero losses is pretty damn impressive, though. Speaking of which, Fay, do you remember when I treated you to tea and cake? I know it was a while ago."

"Sure I do," Fay said. It had been back when he was a freshly minted rookie. Miranda had rented out the dining hall to throw a welcome party for him and the other new apostles, who were all still getting over their rookie jitters.

"How was the cake at that party?" Miranda asked.

"It was okay, I guess."

"It was *the best*, right?" Miranda said.

"Huh? Er... Well, if you say so. I don't remember that clearly, but yeah, it was pretty good."

"Exactly! That's what I'm trying to tell you!"

Fay still wasn't sure *what* she was trying to tell him.

"The Ruin branch office took you under its wing and brought you up from your first days as a rookie, Fay! I'd say you owe us a little something for that, wouldn't you?"

"Uh, s-sure..."

"You wouldn't sell out your beloved home branch office, would you? After the WGT's over, there's not going to be any *Well, the pay's better, so I think I'll stay at* this *office* business, right? You would never, ever be so inhuman, would you? The Ruin branch office is the best, isn't it?!"

"You're scaring me! C-calm down, Chief Secretary. I promise, when the WGT is over, I'll come back here."

"Good! Now I can rest easy." Miranda finally started to calm herself. Only for a second, though—the next moment, she was pulling some paperwork out of a desk drawer. "If I could get your signature on this contract saying so. Just as a formality."

"Exactly how worried are you about us leaving?! I'll come back—you don't have to make me sign a contract!"

So it was that Fay, the Dragon God Leshea, and Pearl (team name TBD) decided to go out into the wider world to be part of the World Games Tournament.

"Umm... Chief Secretary Miranda?" Pearl raised a trembling hand. "This means we'll be going to another city, right? And you said there were lots of cities that wanted us."

"That's right. To be precise, as of this moment, there have been requests from twenty-one separate Arcane Court branch offices."

"So which one do we go to?" Twenty-one places scattered all over the world? They'd never have time to visit them all. "It's our first time at this...this WGT. Maybe we could narrow it down to one or two candidates. The question is how. Is there anywhere you want to go, Fay?"

"You can settle it with darts for all I care," Miranda said. "It would be nice and fair."

Darts: a game of throwing tiny arrows at a round target. The only problem was that neither Fay nor Leshea would ever miss their throw. They could practically choose whatever city they wanted. Not very fair. No, to keep things equal, someone else was needed.

"Maybe someone not very good at darts," Miranda mused.

"Pearl, why don't you toss?" Fay suggested.

"I can't shake the sense that I'm being insulted...but all right. I, Pearl, accept the honor of selecting the city for our tour!" She got ready to throw, focusing on the dartboard on the office wall with the utmost concentration.

"All right. Ready," Miranda said. She'd covered the dartboard in small sticky notes, one to each segment of the board. The Sacred Spring City of Mal-ra. The Volcano City of Voldanra. The Ocean City of Fisshara. The names were there. Now Pearl's dart would decide their destination. "Anywhere you like, my dear Pearl."

"Okay!" Pearl swung the dart above her head and prepared to fling it as hard as she could. Her form was all wrong, but before Fay could point that out, she cried, "Hwaachaa!" and let it fly.

The dart lodged firmly in the sticky note labeled SACRED SPRING CITY OF MAL-RA.

"Is that good, Chief Secretary?" Pearl asked.

"Hm? Oh, Mal-ra? It's as good as anywhere else. Not far away, either." She was studying the dart's target with interest. "Word is they got a highly capable rookie in the year before last. Might be a kindred spirit for you and Lady Leshea, Fay. Have fun!"

"Huh... Do you know anything about this apostle?" Fay asked.

"Not much. But it didn't take long for everyone in Mal-ra to start talking about him, so he's probably a pretty good player." She spun the dart expertly atop her pointer finger, the corners of her lips coming up in a grin. "By the way, Fay, there's an unspoken rule that comes with any friendly encounter between branch offices. Do you know what it is?"

"Er, no."

*"Losing is not an option."*

# 2

Much of this world remained terra incognita to humanity. Take one step outside the cities, and you were in the territory of the Rexes, massive, primitive creatures that roamed the open field. Or you could be in a scorching desert that would desiccate a human body in less than an hour. If it weren't for the metal walls surrounding the human settlements, hordes of Rexes would have leveled the cities overnight. It all boiled down to one thing: getting to another city meant taking your life in your hands.

"I have nothing but respect for the apostles from the old days," Pearl said, looking out the window. They were riding a special-express train on the Continental Railroad, which connected the cities together. In her hand, Pearl held four playing cards. "The way they used their Arise powers after they'd retired to guard the cities and make slow but steady inroads into the territory around them."

"Huh," Leshea said without much interest. She plucked one of the cards from Pearl's hand. They were playing old maid. "You mean they were exploring uncharted areas and stuff?"

"Uh-huh. You know how the gods give Arises to us apostles? A teleportation ability like mine isn't very useful in exploration, but apostles with Superhuman powers or mages with offensive magic, they can do all kinds of good. Exploring is dangerous business, you know."

People needed power if they were going to survive out in merciless nature. Power for blazing new frontiers in this world. The Arises bestowed by the gods were the answer to humanity's prayers.

**(From) The Seven Rules of the Gods' Games**
**Rule 1: Humans granted an Arise by the gods become apostles.**
**Rule 2: Those with an Arise will receive either a Super-human or a Magical power.**
**Rule 5: However, as a reward for obtaining victory in the gods' games, a partial measure of an Arise power may be manifested within the real world. Further victories will unlock greater expressions of the ability.**

There were "Superhumans" with the ability to outrun a Rex. Mages whose ice magic could chill the scorching blaze of the desert wind, or whose wind spells could blow a massive aquatic creature right out of the ocean.

"Humans and gods both get something out of it," Fay said, putting his two cents in, even as he took the rightmost of the cards Leshea was holding up for him. "By granting Arises to humans, the gods get to pass the time playing all the games they want, while humans gain some ability to explore the outside world." That was the gods' games in a nutshell. The most thrilling entertainment known to humankind—and the means to gain power they needed to survive beyond the city walls.

"Come on, Pearl!" Leshea said, leaning toward her. She pointed to the three cards lying facedown on Pearl's leg. "Keep the game moving!"

"Eep! Sorry... I got so caught up in chatting... R-right. It's my turn, isn't it?" She swept up her cards, grabbing the rightmost card from Fay's hand.

As she looked at the card, her eyebrow gave a single, solitary twitch. Leshea noticed immediately. "Say, Pearl?"

"Y-yes?! What is it, Leshea?"

"I'm curious," she said. Her lips were curling into a smile, but her eyes were grim. In fact, she had Pearl fixed with an intense stare. "Why do you look so glum? Aren't you enjoying the game?"

"I-I'm smiling! I'm smiling so hard!"

"Why is your voice cracking?"

"O-o-o-oh, is there a c-c-crack in my voice?!"

"And your fingers, the ones holding your cards..."

"If you think they're shaking, they're not!" Pearl howled, loud enough to earn a look from the mother and child a few seats over. "I'll have you know, Leshea, that your little mind games won't work on me! You don't have the slightest evidence that I just drew the joker!"

"Really? I'd say I have loads."

"What?! No! The card I took from Fay was just an unremarkable, perfectly ordinary—"

"Joker," Fay volunteered.

"Fay, how could you?!" Pearl cried. "Wh-why would you tell her that? It's against the rules to say who drew what card in old maid!"

"We all know by now. It's not really giving anything away." It was only the three of them playing. Pearl had drawn the Joker from Fay, so of course he knew she had it. But then, so did Leshea—because Fay had taken it from her. "I drew the Joker from Leshea and put it in my hand. You immediately grabbed it, so I'm pretty sure Leshea knows which card you took." Only Pearl hadn't been watching where Fay put his card. Because...

*"Come on, Pearl! Keep the game moving!"*

*"Eep! Sorry..."*

...she'd been busy picking up her cards. That had been the same instant Fay had drawn from Leshea's hand.

"You've got a habit, Pearl. You usually take the card on your right, or else the second from your right," Fay said.

"Huh?" Pearl said.

"In the past five games, you've drawn forty-eight times, and you've selected one of those twenty-three times. That means about every other draw. I thought if I kept the joker to your right, maybe you'd take it from me."

"I...I do that? So that's why I've been having such rotten luck!"

In fact, Pearl had one more tell: whenever she drew the joker, she blinked twice. A behavior deeply embedded in her subconscious that seemed intended to relax her, to relieve some anxiety.

*But maybe I'll keep that one to myself for a while yet. It's fun to watch her*, Fay thought.

Pearl mused, "I've been meaning to ask, Fay. This 'Sacred Spring City' we've been invited to—Mal-ra. Are the three of us the only ones who are going to take on the gods' games there?"

"Nah. There'll be participants from the local branch office, too. At least according to Chief Secretary Miranda." The gods' games took the form of encounters between one god and several humans. They would need more than just the three of them to have a successful match. "I wouldn't be surprised if some of the people in Mal-ra want to join us to play games, too."

"That's...," Pearl said.

"As for us, we need teammates, right? We can't keep partnering with different teams every time forever." In an ideal scenario, Fay would have a team that could tackle the gods' games all on their own. He would need about ten people—but he couldn't just go adding members willy-nilly. "They need to be in tune with us. We need to work well together. And like I said before, it would be great if they had versatile Arises. Like you, Pearl."

"Versatile! Wow! I'm thrilled to hear you say that, even if I do know you're just flattering me."

"I'm not flattering anyone. I mean it."

Pearl Diamond was a Teleporter, someone with the ability to

change location instantaneously. Pearl referred to her Arise as "The Wandering," and it gave her two distinct abilities. One was simple teleportation; she could open two warp portals anywhere within a thirty-meter radius and move freely between them. The other was called a "Shift Change." It swapped the locations of any two people or objects, with the proviso that in the past three minutes said person or object had either passed through one of Pearl's warp portals, or Pearl herself had touched them.

*Most Teleporters would have one or the other—but Pearl has both*, Fay thought. Used correctly, that could be enough to help them snatch victory in one of the gods' games. Or put another way, with someone as capable as Pearl on their team, the bar for prospective teammates got that much higher.

"Imagine if we drew an athletic game, like tag or a marathon. You and I are both pretty hopeless at those, right? Wouldn't it be nice to have a teammate we knew could come through in a match like that? You know, a Superhuman! That reminds me, Pearl, I never asked. Who would you like to have on the team? Like, what sort of person sounds ideal to you? Or what are your dealbreakers?"

"What? Wh-who do *I* want? Hrmm..." Pearl crossed her arms in thought, inadvertently displaying her cards to the other two. She didn't seem to notice. "I don't have any preferences when it comes to the type of Arise. But I'm kind of a scaredy-cat, so maybe we could avoid people with frightening faces or who shout a lot. What about you, Leshea?"

"Me? I'm open to anyone who loves games! Except... Hmm." Leshea was staring straight ahead. That is, she was looking at Pearl, who was sitting across from her—but her penetrating gaze was not fixed on Pearl's face. Instead, she was eyeing the two prodigious mounds currently emphasized by Pearl's crossed arms. "Women who are large in one particular area are absolutely not allowed on my team."

"What exactly are you looking at?!" Pearl cried.

"Your pectorals," Leshea said.

"You were checking out my *muscles*?!"

Their banter was interrupted by a ringing from the little pouch Leshea carried.

They heard the chief secretary on the other end of the line. "Good morning, Lady Leoleshea."

"Oh, Miranda. Hey."

"I assume you caught the train to Mal-ra safely? You didn't wind up on the wrong one, did you?"

"Oh, of course we're on the right train. Fay told us what to do."

"Excellent. That's good to hear." There was a short pause, and then Miranda cleared her throat. "I know I wasn't keen on this idea the other day, but after giving it some thought, I think the WGT could be an excellent opportunity for you, Lady Leshea."

"How so?"

"A crash course in human society." Miranda sounded very serious indeed. "I know how much studying you've done, but this is your chance to go beyond the books. To see what's out there with your own eyes. Consider it a study trip. And a chance not only to deepen your knowledge, but also your connection with Fay."

Fay pointed at himself as if to say, *Me?* The conversation was already moving on, however. "Now, Lady Leshea. You'll have some time on your hands during the train ride. What have you been doing? Don't tell me the three of you have spent the entire trip playing cards or board games."

"Yeah, cards," Leshea said, but she cocked her head. "Do you think we should have played something else? What's your recommendation, Miranda?"

"My recommendation is that you don't waste all your time on the train playing around! You need to have some pointless, meandering conversations! You're at an age when boys and girls should spend their time chatting about love and romance!"

"Love and romance?"

"Listen to me, Lady Leshea!" The chief secretary was really warming to her subject now. "I grant that you, Fay, and Pearl have excellent teamwork, but you lack something as a team: trust."

"We have tons of trust," Leshea said.

"Wrong! Your teamwork within the games is dictated by your intimacy in daily life outside them. You can't neglect real life!"

"Intimacy?"

"That's right. There's more to life than games. The WGT could be a fantastic opportunity for you and Fay to get to know each other. It's a change from daily routine, a city you've never been to—you might both see new sides of each other. And you might just find your hearts growing closer."

"I see! Yeah, I get it!" Leshea stood up, still holding the communications device. What Miranda was saying must have really struck a chord because her eyes were shining. "It matters so much that Fay and I learn to be real friends!"

"Now you're getting the idea! You have to think and feel as one in order for the two of you to be perfect partners. For example, when Fay takes a bath, I strongly recommend you jump in with him. You can press right up against him and coo 'Let me wash your back for you...'"

"I'll do it!"

"Don't do that!" Fay interjected, but Leshea was too excited to hear him.

"Then when he gets out of the bath, you wrap yourself around him from behind and whisper, 'Oops, I'm dizzy.' Then the two of you tumble into bed together like good friends do. Now, that's a winning strategy! No better way for you and Fay to get in sync!"

"Th-that's *indecent*!" cried Pearl. Whatever she was imagining, her face was red as a cherry. (Fay was simply speechless by this point.) "F-for a boy and a girl our age to share a bed...

There's no way they could go a whole night without something happening! As their teammate, I won't allow it!"

"Oh, really? Are you telling me you can't let anyone get the jump on you, Pearl?" They could practically hear the grin on the chief secretary's face. "You look so demure and mature, but it turns out you're quite the schemer. So you're planning to somehow hold Lady Leshea back while using your inordinate physical gifts to steal Fay away from her?"

"No! My Fay!" Leshea exclaimed.

"You can't just *lie* about someone like that!" Pearl's voice could be heard all around the train car. "Y-yes, of course I owe Fay a lot, and as a fellow apostle I think he's a wonderful person and have nothing but respect for him…"

"Pearl, Pearl. Don't you think it would be a beautiful thing if you were to take a step further than that?"

"Hrk!"

"It's hardly unusual for apostles to find themselves feeling something deeper than camaraderie for their teammates. Some might even say it's only natural. It's very important to be honest about your feelings."

Pearl was silent for a moment, gazing at the ceiling, looking like she was in the grip of romance. After a moment she mumbled, "I have to confess, it…it's not *impossible*…"

"PEARRRL!" Leshea bellowed, her hackles raised.

Pearl dove for the next train car. "I was talking to myself, I swear!"

Watching them, Fay heard laughter from the communications device. "Ah ha ha! Nice to know you're having a good time, Fay. I was only teasing, but it sounds like there might just be something in the air!"

"Yeah, no comment," Fay said, turning away from the girls.

**Pearl**

Are you all packed for the WGT, Leshea? We can't come back if you forget anything.

**Leshea**

Sure am! I stuffed every game I could into my bag!

**Pearl**

I don't mean games!

I mean… We're going to be there for a while. You have money and enough clothes and your toothbrush? And your favorite pillow?

**Leshea**

I'll just borrow yours.

**Pearl**

You could at least try to bring your own!

**Leshea**

Huh?! Wait, I see. You're saying the bust on your bras is too large for me.

That's why you can't lend them to me!

**Pearl**

That's not what I'm saying at all!

# Player.2
## Join My Team! / Let Me Join Your Team!

# 1

Dawn was breaking. After an entire night's travel on the Continental Railroad, a city skyline was just coming into view on the horizon—the Sacred Spring City of Mal-ra. After a long journey through the scorching wilderness, the train finally arrived.

"We made it!" Pearl said, practically tumbling out the train door.

"Yeah, we're finally here!" Leshea emerged behind her, eyes gleaming. "So this is the Sacred Spring City of Mal-ra. I wonder what the most famous local game is. We'd better start by hitting up the game shops!" She was raring to go. Glancing back at Fay, she yelled, "Let's get going, Fay!"

"Er, yeah. I guess it's all right. We've got some time until we're supposed to be at the Mal-ra branch office this afternoon."

"Say, Fay," Pearl whispered, gesturing toward the main exit just beyond the wicket. "Who do you suppose that is?"

Standing there was a tall girl with an athletic physique and lustrous black hair. The sleeves of her plain shirt were rolled up to her shoulders, revealing powerful, toned biceps. Fay guessed she was his age, or maybe a year older. She looked mature, grown-up somehow, but there was still a girlish innocence in her eyes.

None of that, however, explained why she'd caught Pearl's attention. "She's a little...odd," Pearl said.

She was odd, all right. Suspicious, even. For one thing, she had a bright red headband wrapped around her forehead like she belonged to some sort of cheerleading squad. The impression was reinforced by the large banners she carried, one in each hand, the kind of thing cheer squads liked to wave around.

"MASTER FAY! LADY PEARL! LADY LEOLESHEA! WELCOME! IT'S SO WONDERFUL TO HAVE YOU IN OUR CITY!" She was conspicuous, to say the least. The passersby who packed the station made it a point to steer clear of her.

"What's her deal?" Even Leshea was brought up short. "Whatever she's doing, I don't get it."

"I've got a bad feeling about this!" Pearl said.

"Shh! It's probably best if she doesn't notice us," Fay said. The three of them looked at each other, silently agreeing to try to avoid the young woman. "Okay. We pretend not to know each other, then we make our escape. Blend into the crowd..."

"Hrm?!" The black-haired girl turned. Had she caught a hint of their voices? Sensed their footsteps? Whatever the case, she was looking directly at them. Her eyes went wide, and she exclaimed, "Ahhhh! I never expected you to be *right here*!"

"Ruuun!" Fay yelled, and they all set off as fast as they could.

He could hear the girl behind them, calling, "W-wait! Why are you running away?! I swear I'm not going to hurt you!"

"That's the least reassuring thing you could possibly say!" Fay shouted back.

"Everything about you says *Don't come near this person!*" Pearl added. They didn't stop running. They were making for the big thoroughfare they could see just ahead.

*          *          *

Then there was a gust of wind.

It was followed by a *whoosh*, and the sound of shoes skidding across asphalt. Fay had barely registered the noise when the young woman overtook them with the speed of a hurricane.

"Uh?" said Pearl, completely dumbfounded. It took a moment to understand what had happened—the young woman had raced past them, so fast she practically left an afterimage in the air.

*Wait, no one should be able to move that fast! We were fifty meters from her, but she covered it in less than two seconds!*

Such speed was well beyond human capabilities—which left just one explanation. She was an apostle with powers granted by the gods. A Superhuman with enhanced physical abilities.

"You're an apostle?" Fay asked.

"Allow me to introduce myself!" said the young woman. She placed a hand to her heart, her hair billowing behind her. "My name is Nel Reckless, former apostle serving in the Sacred Spring City of Mal-ra!"

"Former?" Something felt off, but before Fay could process what this girl Nel was saying, she was speaking again—and what she said next made them all freeze.

"Master Fay, I want you to make me your woman!"

There was a very long pause, after which Fay mumbled, "Huh?" He had never made such an earnest sound of befuddlement in his life.

*"Your woman"*? It was the strangest request he'd ever heard.

"......"

"......"

Pearl and Leshea were both staring at him. Leshea looked particularly shocked; Fay hadn't realized her eyes could get that big.

"Hm?" Nel said. Then she put her hands together. "Oh! I

don't mean that in, you know, a *weird* way! I just want to work for you."

"And that's how you tell me?! I was about to run off again!"

"Master Fay!" Nel shouted, her voice resounding around the street. "When I saw the stream of you fighting Uroboros, I knew. I knew you were the master I was destined to serve! I beg you to admit me to your service!"

"Service? Master? Maybe we could cut down on the hyperbole..."

"It's not hyperbole!" Nel's voice went up an octave and her face flushed with excitement. They were attracting looks and chatter, but Nel was so fixated on him that she hardly seemed to notice.

Instead, Fay said, "I, uh...I think people are starting to notice your shouting..."

"I'll cook for you! Do your laundry! Iron your clothes! I-I'll even wash your back in the bath, if you so desire!"

"Maybe don't say that in public!" Fay choked. Damn. It was obvious that once the blood went to this dark-haired girl's head, she stopped caring who was around to hear her. "Sigh... Geez. Look, I've got no idea what's going on. Right, Leshea? ...Leshea?"

Fay turned to discover Leshea and Pearl having a whispered conversation, stormy expressions on their faces.

"Fay," Leshea said. "To think, when you have a being like *me* with you..."

"Yes, Fay! Telling a girl you've never met to wash your back and do your cooking and launder your clothes... I'm not sure I can continue to defend a man like that!" Pearl said.

"This is exactly what I need defending *from*!" Fay cried, but there was no time to talk things out. Nel was already striding up behind him.

"Be my master, I beg you!" she said.

"I told you, I'm not anyone's master!"

"You say you want me to grovel in the dust?! Then I shall!"

"I didn't say that! Wait...you're really gonna do it?!"

Right there on the crowded street, Nel knelt down and ground her forehead into the asphalt. It was fantastic groveling. "Behold!" she cried.

Fay was speechless.

"Master Fay!"

She was greeted by silence. She waited and waited, but she heard nothing. Puzzled, she slowly looked up...

...to see Fay and his companions running away as fast as they could.

"Ahhh! Wait! Wait, Mas—"

Nel was about to go running after them when chatter broke out around her. A horn blared. "Look out!" someone shouted.

"Get out of the way, miss! That car's gonna—"

The driver of the truck currently turning through the inter-section had never in his wildest dreams expected to find a young girl prostrating herself in the middle of the street. He slammed on the brakes when he saw Nel, but it was much too late.

She was going to get run over. Everyone froze in terror. Everyone, that is, except Nel.

"Yah!" She kicked off the street with her left foot, lifting her right at the same time, and began to spin like a top. Her foot con-nected with the oncoming truck at incredible speed. There was a burst of light where she struck the vehicle.

Her Arise activated.

Nel Reckless had a Superhuman power—one that enhanced her legs.

Moment Reversal: anything Nel kicked would be pushed away from her, no matter the amount of energy involved. Be it a falling asteroid or an incoming missile, as long as she got the

timing right, there was nothing she couldn't kick away. A truck
was child's play for her.

"Oh—!" Nel cried. The truck was sent barreling backward,
its speed undiminished, straight into a wall. It toppled over and
came to rest on its side in a cloud of smoke. "Oh... Oh no! I didn't
mean to! It's just a reflex! D-driver! Are you okay?!" she said,
clutching her head with her hands. By that time, Fay and the
others were long gone.

# 2

They arrived at the Arcane Court Mal-ra branch office, a gleaming, bluish-silver tower. As they gazed up at it, the first words out
of Pearl's mouth were: "Huff... Huff... I'm so huuungry!" Followed by: "Wh-who was that girl? And what was her problem?"

"I think we lost her," Fay said. He wiped sweat off his brow.
Maybe it was the pounding sun. "I don't have any answers for
you, but I'm pretty sure running away was the right choice."

They'd fled from the dark-haired girl named Nel—Fay
assumed she was a Superhuman apostle—then kept running,
and before they knew it, they were here. So much for their plan
to look around town a little and get some lunch first.

"Aww... I needed that time to eat," Pearl groaned.

"Arrgh... My game-shop crawl!" Leshea griped.

"All right, you two, here we go," Fay said, taking his despon-
dent companions by their hands and pulling them toward the
entrance. As soon as they stepped inside, they found themselves
in what looked like it could have been the lobby of a museum. For
one thing, they were greeted by a giant statue of a god.

"Ooh. Undine, the Water Spirit, huh?" Fay said. This spirit
was the legendary guardian of the Sacred Spring City of Mal-ra.
As he stood admiring the statue, a buzz began behind him,

spreading through the large hall. The talk came from Mal-ra's apostles. They wore the same uniforms as Fay and his friends, but the trim on their shoulders was red. The Ruin outfits had blue shoulders, making it obvious that Fay and the others were visitors.

"Uh! I think we've been noticed, Fay," Pearl said.

"Uh-huh. And why are you hiding behind me, exactly?"

"I hate being noticed!"

"I'm not—"

—*such a fan of it myself,* he was about to say, but he was interrupted by a burly man who put a hand on Pearl's shoulder. "You three," the man said.

"Eep?" Pearl said.

His hand was so big, he looked like he could have casually crushed a watermelon with it. Pearl turned to find the man looking down at her—at least, she thought he was, though his sunglasses made it hard to tell.

"Are you by any chance—" he started, but he was interrupted by Pearl shouting, "CREEP!" She disappeared, teleporting herself back to the entrance of the lobby. She pointed an accusing finger at the large man. "Security! Mr. Security Guard! This man is a pervert!"

"No, I'm not!"

"Then what were you doing touching my shoulder?!"

"I was just getting your attention..."

"Now I *know* he's a pervert!"

"I'm the chief secretary here!"

"Wha?" Pearl blinked.

The man, who had short cropped golden hair and was wearing a jacket, shrugged in frustration. "Welcome to the Mal-ra branch of the Arcane Court. I'm the chief secretary, Baleggar Ions."

\*　　\*　　\*

Two minutes later, Fay and his companions were heading up the floors of the Mal-ra branch office on their way to Baleggar's office.

By the stairs.

"Um… Why exactly are we taking the stairs?" Pearl asked.

"Because the chief secretary's office is on the eighth floor," Fay said.

"N no, I mean… I'm pretty sure there was an elevator right there."

"This is better for your health," the chief secretary replied without looking back. He was climbing ahead of them, his broad back and rippling muscles guiding them up the stairs. "Walking promotes blood flow, which gets more oxygen to your brain. More oxygen to the brain means sharper thinking, which means smarter gameplay. That's why physical training is so important!"

"Aww," Pearl said.

From behind her, Leshea exclaimed, "What a great philosophy!" She was bounding up the stairs two at a time. As they reached a landing—quite quickly, in her case—she said, "Healthy play comes from a healthy body! I couldn't agree more!"

"I'm honored that you see things my way, Lady Dragon God Leoleshea."

"Of course! Better physical conditioning means you can play longer. Pearl, you'd better be sure you train your game muscles!"

"Game muscles?!"

"Those are the muscles you use when you play a game!"

"I don't know which muscles those are!"

"All right," Chief Secretary Baleggar said, never pausing his trek up the stairs nor turning around. "I was going to wait until we were in the office to discuss this, but I'm sure you're all busy people. Let me tell you a little bit about the event while we get up these stairs. First of all, allow me to extend my gratitude to you for choosing our city as your destination for the World Games Tour."

"We could have been at the eighth floor already if we'd taken the elevator," Pearl moaned.

"As I believe you know, what we want is for you to use one of the Divine Gates here in Mal-ra to take on the gods' games. We've got extensive support facilities ready to go, and we sold out the city's sports stadium. I can guarantee that at least ten thousand people will be watching you play."

"Ten thousand people?! You sold every ticket?" Pearl asked.

"I tell you, the people of Mal-ra will be cheering so loud you'll be able to hear them on the other side of the gate. And of course, we'll be livestreaming the proceedings around the world."

"Y-yikes... I'm not so sure about this, Fay..." Pearl poked him in the back. She was white as a sheet; she looked like she was in the grip of the panic to end all panics.

"I also see this as a chance to foster friendship between our cities. Many of our apostles have been waiting on the edge of their seats for your visit. Lots of people are more than excited to play with you. A lovely opportunity for a friendly intercity battle. I hope you'll agree."

The WGT had two parts. The main event was the gods' game to be played in three days. But tomorrow, they would have this "friendly" battle.

"We were absolutely flooded with applicants who wanted to be part of the intercity match. People who wanted to test themselves against a former god like Lady Leoleshea, and Fay, one of the most celebrated rookies in recent memory."

"Huh?" Pearl said, snapping back to reality. "So what about me? Does that mean that I..." She began to blush happily. "I mean, of course! It makes sense. After all, I *did* defeat the undefeated god, Uroboros. I shouldn't be surprised if every apostle in the world knows who I am now. Hee-hee!"

Nobody said anything.

"Why the total silence?! Ch-chief Secretary? What about *my* popularity?!" Her plaintive cries echoed around the staircase, and when they faded away there was still no answer.

The eighth-floor office was covered in dozens and dozens of photographs. They all showed apostles, but each seemed to wear a different uniform.

"These are commemorative photos from last year's WGT. The next ones are from the year before that. These group photos all show apostles who participated as guests from other cities," Baleggar said.

Leshea was looking at the photos with interest. "Huh. Their clothes are all different colors. I never really thought much about it before." Each branch office of the Arcane Court had a different color uniform, and Leshea seemed to be drinking in every outfit in every photo in the display. "Oh, Fay! What's this one?" she said, pointing at the last picture. It showed a four-person group of apostles, guys and girls, but it was probably their outfits that had attracted her attention: they were all black. Unlike the clothing worn by Fay and the other apostles, which was mostly white, these four wore imposing black uniforms with gold embroidery.

"That's not normal, is it?" Leshea said.

"Oh, that's a team who's received a rank of AA or better from the Arcane Court," Fay said. "That's not easy. There's stiff criteria, including your win ratio in the gods' games, how your team is managed, and other stuff too. Most teams, it's all they can do to get an A rank."

There was perhaps one team at each office that might merit the rank of AA. Which meant, in essence, that the best team at each office was entitled to wear black vestments. What caught Fay's eye, however, was the golden embroidery. "Look at this, Leshea. See how the trim on their shoulders is in gold? That would mean they're..."

"Headquarters," said Chief Secretary Baleggar. "The black outfits mean simply that they're the most accomplished team at their office; they could be from anywhere. But that golden thread, that's different. Only members of Arcane Court headquarters are allowed to wear that, Lady Leoleshea."

"Huh?"

"I believe there were several messengers sent from head-quarters when you were dug out of your glacier about a year ago, weren't there?"

"I sure don't remember any."

"These are the ones who sent them. This photo is from when they came to our city at the behest of the Arcane Court." Chief Secretary Baleggar slid his sunglasses up the bridge of his nose and looked at the picture of the four apostles in black and gold.

"This is the representative team from Arcane Court head-quarters, Mind Over Matter," he said. (Their motto: "The Holy See where all souls gather.")

Headquarters' representatives. In other words, the strongest team in the entire world.

"Hmm..." Leshea looked less than convinced, but her eyes sparkled when she heard that they were accomplished game players. "Something's different about them. Something's off."

"What do you mean, Leshea?" Fay asked.

"Well—"

*Clack-clack-clack.* She was cut off by the sharp rap of shoes on the floor.

"I haven't seen those uniforms around here before. Blue trim... The Ruin branch office?"

Another apostle had entered the hall. His hair was silver—nearly dark gray, and his eyes radiated intensity and strength. His face was as gorgeous as any actor's, and his physical fitness indicated long hours of physical training.

"Are these our much-anticipated guests, Chief Secretary?" he asked.

Baleggar turned to him. "Oh, Dax. I should have known you would want to greet our guests even before the competition. Well, your timing is perfect. Lady Leoleshea, allow me to introduce—"

"Dax," said the young man. His voice was foreboding—and his uniform was black. "Dax Gear Scimitar. I joined the Mal-ra branch office two years ago. And I've heard a great deal about you lot."

"Dax! Watch your tone! You're in the presence of a former—"

"I'm not inclined to offer any special treatment," he said, brushing off Baleggar's protest. "I don't care what she *used* to be. I only care if she's any good at games."

"Well!" The corners of Leshea's mouth turned up and she flipped her vermilion hair out of her eyes with a quick sweep of her hand. "That's good to hear. I like your type—humans who only have eyes for games."

"Umm, Chief Secretary?" Pearl asked, looking puzzled. "You said this young man was a rookie the year before last, but he's wearing a black outfit. Which would mean..."

"Exactly what you think it does." Baleggar nodded. He pointed at the young man, Dax. "He established his own team just nine months after his debut, faster than anyone on record. They took victory in their first game against the gods. To date, he's racked up a record of three wins, one loss. In just a single

year, his team became the representatives of the Mal-ra branch office. And he's the one who started it all."

"Really?! His own team, after barely a year with the Arcane Court?!"

"That's right. It was unheard of. I have to admit, it's not what I would have chosen as chief secretary. But his results spoke for themselves." Baleggar sighed. "Dax here *is* the top of the heap at our office."

"Th-that's amazing. He's almost like—" Pearl stopped and clapped her hands over her mouth. To Fay, however, it was obvious that she had been about to say, *"He's almost like Fay."* Their situations were nearly identical: they'd beaten the gods as rookies and elevated themselves enough to be seen as the chief representatives of their respective branch offices.

Those weren't the only similarities, either. Dax, like Fay, showed no fear of Leshea; he, too, was focused entirely on games. Fay had never imagined that there would be another rookie out there quite as skilled and quite as unique as he was.

"Fay Theo Philus," Dax said, stepping forward with a sweep of his black coat. "Truly, you and I have been brought together by destiny!"

"Excuse me?" Fay said.

"I saw your matches on the livestreams. You deserve praise for your performance in Titan's game of Divinitag, and of course in Uroboros's Forbidden Word."

"Huh? Oh, uh, thanks." The compliment sort of caught him off guard. Fay didn't love the tone of condescension, but the guy just seemed to be that way. "That's nice of you to say and everything, but 'destiny' is kind of a big word to be throwing around—"

"Therefore, I say unto you: come to my team!"

After a very, very long pause, Fay managed to respond,

"*Excuse* me?" What did Dax think he was saying? Leshea and Pearl looked as confused as Fay felt. Only Chief Secretary Baleggar didn't look surprised; he heaved a sigh.

"I'm recruiting the best rookies from around the world. We will surpass even *them*!" Dax turned, his gaze alighting on the central photo of the four apostles. "Headquarters thinks their precious Mind Over Matter is the strongest team around, but I will go beyond them to create the *true* strongest team in history! And then we will clear the gods' games!" He thrust out his right hand. *What? Did he think he was in a movie or something?* "I saw the calm, calculating strategy you deployed in your game with Titan. And the fortitude of spirit with which you went up against Uroboros. Fay! You are the final piece that I seek!" Fay didn't answer, so Dax kept talking: "Come with me. Together, we shall form the strongest team the world has ever known!"

Silence fell in the great hall. Dax, ambition burning in his eyes, looked at Fay. Fay looked back at Dax and said...

"Hey, Pearl."

"Wh-what?! Yes?!"

"Lotta *interesting* apostles in this city, huh?" His expression softened. No sooner had he arrived in Mal-ra than he'd received two completely opposite requests.

*"I beg you to admit me to your service!"*
*"Come to my team!"*

The brunette girl, Nel, had begged to join Fay's team, while Dax was inviting Fay to join his.

"Thanks, but I'm afraid I'm gonna have to turn you down," Fay said with a glance at Leshea and Pearl, then a shrug at Dax. The two women watched him closely. "We're here for the WGT. Not to join anyone's team."

"I see."

"Er... Huh? That's all you have to say?"

"My business here is finished." The silver-haired young man turned on his heel and strode away. His response was so anticlimactic that it was Fay who was left feeling like the wind had been taken out of his sails.

"Yeah... Lotta interesting people," he repeated, watching Dax go with an uneasy smile. "Especially since that didn't look like the face of a guy who'd given up."

# 3

The night scenery twinkled twenty floors below as Fay looked out from his guestroom in the Arcane Court Mal-ra branch office. "Huh! I wonder if that big domed building is the stadium they were talking about. They said spectator tickets sold out in seven minutes...

There was a distinct *crack* as someone twisted open the handle of his door, which was supposed to be locked. "All right, Fay! Time for some fun!" Leshea bounded in, dressed in her casual clothes. "We're gonna play!" She was holding a board game under her arm.

"I even made dinner for you," said Pearl, carrying a silver tray as she followed Leshea in. "Tomorrow's the intercity competition! I made you a hearty dinner, so you'll have plenty of energy to help us claim victory!"

"Wow, really? Gosh, thanks. That must have been a lot of work."

"It was no trouble—I'm an excellent cook! Ta-da!" She whipped the cover off the tray and fragrant steam wafted through the room. "It's Pearl's special sandwich! A ten-centimeter hamhock burger wrapped in bacon wrapped in cheese!"

"That's the meatiest sandwich I've ever heard of!" In fact, he thought *ham-burger* would have been a more appropriate word. It was pretty much just a pile of meat! It looked too thick to even fit in his mouth—but Pearl was puffing her chest out proudly.

"You need energy if you're going to fight! And where do you get energy? Protein!"

"Are there even any vegetables on this thing?"

"There's two lettuce leaves tucked in there."

"This is not a balanced meal! But...since you went through the trouble of making it, I guess I'll have some..." Fay took a bite. "Huh? This is...surprisingly edible. In fact, it's pretty good!"

"Hee-hee! I thought so. The trick is to use spices like black pepper and cloves to neutralize the oiliness and keep the smell from being overwhelming while retaining the meat's umami! Then you toss in a few small slices of dried orange to give it that fresh zest."

"Gosh. I never knew you had this side to you," Fay said, genuinely surprised. True, she'd told him when they met that her hobbies included "making nourishing meals," but he'd never imagined she meant it quite like this.

"Hee-hee! This is a new experience, Fay, hearing you talk about me like that." There was a shy smile on Pearl's face. "See, Leshea? Fay has nice things to say about me, too."

"Huh," said the vermilion-haired young woman standing beside her. There was danger in her eyes, and she wasn't trying to hide it. "I see. So that's what it was."

"Leshea?" Pearl said.

"I wondered what you were so busy with. It's just like Miranda said: our team has to be intimate outside of the games as well as within them. I see what you're aiming at, Pearl!"

"Wh-wh-what? I'm what?! Wh-what in the world do you mean?!"

"I find it very suspicious how shocked you're acting right now."

"I'm not acting shocked! And I'm not aiming at anything yet!"

"*Yet?*"

"A slip of the tongue, I swear!" Pearl fled to a corner of the living room.

Leshea, meanwhile, rounded on Fay. "And you, Fay!"

"Hrk?!" he said, nearly choking on his sandwich. "I mean, uh, Leshea? She put in time and effort to make me dinner. It would be really mean to say I don't want it, right? A homemade meal from a teammate?"

"Oh, yes. Believe me, I know." Leshea's eyes were cold. "That's the way it's been ever since the time of the ancient magical civilization. One of their sages said, 'Men are beholden to two things: well-endowed women and the food such women make.'"

"This was a *sage* who said this?!"

"I see you're no different. You like a girl who can cook, *don't* you?"

"Is there any way to answer that won't result in you getting even angrier? Argh... No, wait!" Fay felt cold sweat trickling down the back of his neck—but then he thought of the one possible exit from this situation. He pointed at the screen on the wall. "This is perfect. I was hoping to show you two something. See the remote on the table, Leshea? Use it to turn on the monitor."

"What, this thing?" Leshea pressed the button on the remote and the monitor came to life. It showed a replay of one of the gods' games.

"Since we're going to be teaming up with apostles from Mal-ra in a couple of days, I figured I should see how they play. And I just happened to spot..."

"Oh! My! *Gosh!*" Pearl yelled, pointing at the screen. "That black-haired girl! I recognize her!"

"Yep. Nel Reckless. The one who staked us out at the station and begged to 'enter my service.'" She'd introduced herself as a *former* apostle, but there was still video of her active tenure. "I looked into it. She only retired a month ago. She had a record of three wins, three losses. A good number, but not amazing."

"R-right..."

"But she's better than the numbers show. I mean it. She really knows what she's doing."

Nel Reckless. Her best genre was real-time strategy (RTS), which demanded snap judgments and quick thinking. Combined with her Superhuman Arise, she would be ideal in an athletic game. Her powerful build and substantial physical gifts made her a joy to watch as she dashed around the field, quick as a gust of wind.

"She does exactly what her team captain tells her to and backs up her friends at every opportunity."

A 3-3 record was not outstanding. But Fay was interested in more than just pure numbers. Luck could always turn against you in the gods' games—for example, someone might get several unfortunate draws in a row, say against a deity like Uroboros.

"Fay," Pearl said, sitting down on the floor and looking intently up at him. "Nel is basically my opposite, right?"

Fay caught his breath.

"I was the reason my own team was defeated, and it bothered me so much that I was going to quit. But Nel..."

Her third loss had been a surrender, a forfeit. She'd wanted to keep playing, but her teammates' spirits had broken before hers.

*"Captain! Vice Captain! Wait! This game isn't over! Three of us are still standing! Please! I don't want it to end this way! It can't end like—"*

\*        \*        \*

She hadn't wanted to give up, but her cries had been over-ruled by majority decision, and she'd been forcibly ejected from Elements. The video ended there.

"Maybe Nel feels like she has unfinished business," Pearl said.

"Could be." Fay leaned against the wall and breathed out a small sigh. He understood her reasons now. Why she'd pursued them so manically that afternoon. Even though she could no longer stand among those who battled with the gods, she wanted to support a team to the best of her abilities.

"I wish she'd told us what was going on. Now I look like the bad guy for running away from her," Fay said, but he couldn't suppress a crooked smile. "And I want to hear more. If I ever see her again, maybe I'll ask her—"

*Ding!* He was interrupted by the ringing of the room's intercom.

"Huh! You think that's Chief Secretary Baleggar?" Pearl said. She got up and opened the door. "Come in, please."

"Room service. I've brought your drinks," said the woman standing at the door. She didn't look like room service, though—she was wearing sunglasses and a face mask, plus a cap on her head.

"Eek!" Pearl yelled, jumping backward. "It's you!"

"Uh, me who? I promise I'm no one suspicious!"

"You're Nel!" It turned out Pearl hadn't been frightened by the visitor's threatening appearance. Instead, the outlandish out-fit had made it all too obvious who the young woman was. Her disguise couldn't hide her distinctive slim, tall figure, and her jet-black hair peeked out from under her hat.

"Nel? What're you doing?" Fay asked.

The girl in the disguise flinched visibly. "N-Nel? Who's Nel? That's not my name..."

"I can tell it's you. I recognize your voice," Fay said.

"Yeah. And your hair," Leshea added.

"Hrrk?! A-aw, shit..." Seeing that she wasn't going to be able to talk her way out of this, Nel looked like she might just abandon her disguise—until she suddenly turned and ran. "See ya!" she shouted.

"Wait—what?!" Fay said, but he couldn't stop her. With her Superhuman ability, she was off down the hallway like a shot.

Fay deflated. "Man...I wanted to talk to her."

---

On the twelfth floor of the Arcane Court office, Nel Reckless leaned against the wall, bracing herself with one hand, her shoulders heaving. "Huff... Puff... Why? Why did I run? Stupid Nel..."

The part-time job as an employee at the Arcane Court had been the perfect opportunity to get close to Fay and his companions. Okay, so the thing that afternoon hadn't worked out so well, but she wanted to ask him at least one more time to let her join his team.

"I can never seem to find my courage when it really counts..."

"Wouldn't have expected you, of all people, to wind up with your tail between your legs."

She heard shoes clicking across the floor. She turned to find a young man in a black uniform standing nearby. "Dax," she said.

"Nel," he replied. They'd co-operated on a game once. "We were assigned to the same cohort a couple of years back. Remember that? Everybody wondered, which of us would come out on top? Well, look at us now."

Nel: three wins, three losses; retired.

Dax: three wins, one loss. Now, he was one of the foremost

apostles at the Mal-ra branch office. His team had practically become Mal-ra's representatives, and many people lauded him as the Prince of Games.

"I've survived while you've retired," Dax said. "What do you suppose is the difference between us? Talent? Skill?"

"You can call it whatever you like."

"It's the *team*."

Nel caught her breath.

"You were unfortunate. Bad luck to wind up with the teammates you did." He tossed something to her. She caught it in midair to find a golden key card glimmering in her hand. She'd seen it before—all the members of team Tempest Cruiser (motto: "At the eye of the world's storm") carried one. And this young man was the team captain. "I think quite highly of your abilities—and your tenacity," Dax said.

"I've heard this song before."

"Yes, you have. And you'll hear it again, as many times as I need to sing it. Join my team, Nel. Become our analyst."

She didn't say anything.

"How long do you intend to squander yourself as another anonymous part-timer here?"

A capable apostle had all sorts of options even after retirement, but the best of all was to contribute to an active team. The saying even went that a good analyst was worth more than a good apostle. Strategy was just that important to the gods' games.

"With you behind us, my team could take another step closer to perfection. To becoming the world's strongest team."

"Nothing doing," Nel said. She didn't even have to think about it. "I have my heart set on joining Master Fay's team. Damned if I'm going anywhere else."

"Why are you so fixated on him?" Dax still appeared every bit the gallant young man; he showed no sign that his feelings had been hurt or his mood impacted. Nel knew he would never be upset simply because his invitation had been rebuffed. It was one of the young man's virtues, almost a special skill. He was the "Prince," with no blemish inside or out. It gave him magnetism—charisma.

It did not, however, draw Nel to him. Her heart had already turned toward Fay. "Call it my intuition," she said. "I believe... I believe Master Fay is the one who can turn *my* dream into reality."

She'd felt it when she saw him play against the Endless God Uroboros.

"Very interesting. In that case"—Dax held out his palm toward her—"how about we make a bet?"

"What?"

"There's a friendly little match planned for tomorrow—my team versus *his*. Cultivating friendship between cities is all well and good but make no mistake: there will be no punches pulled in the showdown between him and me."

He looked at her, brimming with confidence. And why shouldn't he be? This was the man who claimed he was going to defeat the world's strongest team. Now he locked eyes with Nel.

"If I should happen to lose tomorrow, I'll admit that your judgment was correct, and as a token of my defeat, I'll do any one thing you ask. Anything at all. But if and when *I* defeat Fay..."

"Then you want me to join your team."

"I see you've got the idea."

If Dax could show that he was truly the strongest rookie by winning the competition, Nel would have no more reason to show any allegiance to Fay.

"Just you make sure you're watching our battle tomorrow, Nel." Dax gave a flourish of his black overcoat and walked out of the room before Nel could find the words to respond, his shoes rapping loudly against the floor.

# Player.3
## Pride Match

# 1

The sun poured through the windows of the guest room on the twelfth floor of the Arcane Court Mal-ra branch office, tugging at Fay's eyelids. He stifled a yawn as he sat up. "Gosh. Is it morning already?" He was on the floor still holding a hand of playing cards. Apparently, he'd crashed in the middle of an all-night game session. "Leshea? Pearl?"

The two girls lay flat on their backs on the bed, asleep. It looked like they'd dropped off around the same time he had.

"Day two... We've got that match with the local team," Fay said.

It would be them versus Dax. When he'd heard that the most celebrated apostle in Mal-ra had personally volunteered to go up against him, Fay was reminded of what Chief Secretary Miranda had said: *Losing is not an option.* Whatever else it might be, this was a proxy battle between branch offices. Reputations were on the line.

"Wonder what kind of game it's going to be," he said. "Anyway, wake up, you two. We're gonna be late."

"Mmnf," mumbled Leshea.

"Zzzzz," snored Pearl. Neither showed any sign of waking up. They both snoozed away with big, happy looks on their faces. "No, thank you. I couldn't eat another bite," Pearl murmured.

"Great... Let's go another round," Leshea said.

"Well, guess I know what each of you are dreaming about. C'mon, Leshea, wake up!" She'd once slept for three millennia straight. If he couldn't get her to open her eyes, she might not come around for a few decades.

"Hmm?" She twitched. Eyes still closed, she flipped over and stretched out her right arm. "Not yet... Playin' poker..."

"In your sleep?"

"Then I raise!"

Somewhere in her dreams, she must have been throwing some more coins into the pot. What she'd actually grabbed, however, wasn't a pile of coins—it was one of the substantial mounds boasted by Pearl, who slept next to her.

"Hmm? These coins...," Leshea muttered.

"Eeeeeek!" Well, at least Pearl was awake. She began thrashing around, Leshea clutching one side of her chest in an iron grip.

"These coins are so soft..."

"L-Leshea! Those aren't... Hngh! Those aren't coins!"

"This one, then!"

"That's not a coin, either!" Pearl howled. Leshea now had a grip on both sides of her chest, and Pearl looked like she might cry. "Save me, Fay! My chastity is in danger!"

"Guess I'll go get ready by myself," Fay said.

"Don't pretend you don't see! Don't go! Nooooo!"

# 2

The stadium was just a ten-minute walk from the Mal-ra branch office. Fay and his companions went through a special staff entrance.

"W-wow! Do you hear that cheering?" Pearl asked, holding a can of juice with both hands as they walked along. "They did say the stadium was sold out. Wh-what are we gonna do?!"

"Come on, Fay, hurry! Hurry!" Leshea skipped straight past them both, racing down the hallway. "I wonder what kind of game they've got planned in such a huge venue!"

"Given how big the place is, I'm guessing it's something where we'll have to run around a lot. Soccer or rugby, you know? Hrm... But do we have enough people for that? Huh, but so what could they—oh!" Almost without meaning to, Fay came to a halt. The staff corridor had been deserted—but now he saw a familiar black-haired girl running toward him at a spectacular speed. "Nel?"

"Huff... Huff... Thank goodness! I m-made it!" She was out of breath, sucking in oxygen. Fay, Pearl, and Leshea looked at her, open-mouthed. She collected herself enough to look right back at them. "Master Fay. You probably know by now that the opponent you're about to face in this 'friendly competition' is Dax. He may have his nose in the air, but his instinctive talent for games is undeniable. Even someone like you is going to have your work cut out for you, sir." Then she clenched her fist. "But I beg you: you must take victory! Otherwise..."

"Huh? Otherwise what?"

"Grr... There's no time. A-anyway, just win, okay? Please? I'll be cheering you on from the spectator seats!" Then she turned on her heel, and before Fay could call out again, she took off.

"So, this human, Nel..." Leshea said. "She came here just to cheer for us?"

"Guess so. She hasn't gotten any better at explaining herself, I can say that much." Fay smiled a bit as he watched her flee around a corner. "I'd sort of resigned myself to being the bad guy in this match, what with us being the visitors. It's nice to know someone's going to be rooting for us."

"That's true." Leshea giggled. Then she started toward the stadium again, her vermilion hair billowing behind her and catching the light. "Now! I wonder what kind of game they have in store for us."

They emerged from the cramped hallway into the vast competition ground of the stadium.

A deafening cheer came from the stands, which were packed with the people of Mal-ra.

The seats surrounded them, a full three hundred and sixty degrees of faces staring down at them. Even Fay had never experienced more than ten thousand people cheering all at once before.

"Wow. Games never make me nervous, but I'm definitely feeling the pressure from this crowd," he said.

"I've been waiting for you, Fay." Standing in the center of the playing field was the young man with silver hair and a black uniform. "We're about to engage in a pride match between our two cities. But I haven't a shred of interest in defending my city's honor. I've come here to test myself as an athlete of games, to pit my spirit against yours in battle!"

Fay didn't reply.

"You have a problem with that?" Dax asked, folding his arms.

"No, no. I'm just kind of wondering, like, is that a compliment? I mean, I'm hoping it is." Fay couldn't hold back an awkward smile. He realized he'd gotten the wrong impression of Dax. The guy might have movie star looks and preen about his popularity, but there was something else. "I thought you were maybe more...cold-blooded. But I'm seeing some real passion here."

"It depends on who I'm playing against. Show me something that makes my soul burn bright!" Against all Fay's expectations, Dax grinned. "It's time to see what we'll be playing. In order to make everything nice and fair, the game has been chosen at random from thousands and thousands of possibilities available in this stadium." He snapped his fingers. "Operator! Start up the chosen game!"

Immediately, there was an electrical thrum, and the ground beneath Fay's feet changed. "An AR image?" he said.

Augmented Reality, or AR, was a technology for projecting manufactured images onto the real world. Fay had been wondering about it since they'd stepped into the stadium. If the place was normally used for soccer or baseball or whatever, he would have expected grass or sand or something underfoot. Instead, the arena had a white concrete surface.

"Huh. So the whole arena is a projector screen," Fay said. The ground had been entirely replaced with an AR projection, dozens of red, silver, and gold squares.

"It's sugoroku!" Fay said. The stadium floor had become a massive board for the classic game. In the air above them, a scoreboard projected by the AR tech read in letters made of light: Card Strategy Sugoroku: Mind Arena.

"Oh! I've heard of this!" Pearl said. "It's a game that can be used in friendly matches between branch offices. But you don't roll dice to advance like you do in normal sugoroku."

Fay was familiar with the name of the game and the very basic rules. It was a version of a game that had actually been played in the gods' games, reworked so that teams of humans could compete against each other.

The game went something like this:

**Basic Rules**
   1. **Except as otherwise stated, this uses the functions of ordinary sugoroku.**
   2. **There are 2 win conditions. A team can win the game by satisfying either of them.**

Condition A: Reach the goal line, located 44 squares past the start.

Condition B: Reduce a member of the other team's life to 0 using traps or magic cards.

3. Each player starts with 20 life and 5 magic cards.
4. Players select a class when the game begins.

Gameplay

1. In lieu of dice, when the game starts, each player chooses a number between 1 and 6.
2. Players take turns, going from the largest number to the smallest. (If 2 or more players have chosen the same number, the player who chose it first goes first.)
3. On their turn, players may take the following 2 actions:

A: Move forward the number of spaces corresponding to the number they chose. An effect occurs based on the color of the square where they land.

Silver: Draw a magic card.

Gold: Draw 2 magic cards.

(Note: When 2 or more players occupy a silver or gold square, they do not draw a card.)

Red: Red squares are trap zones. Players who land on these squares suffer damage. Damage from traps may not be reduced.

B. Use any number of magic cards.

Self-Applied Magic: May only be used on your own turn, not on an opponent's turn.

High-Speed Magic: Can be used anytime. However, effects are frequently weak or can only be used under very specific conditions.

> **Secret Spells:** Powerful trump cards. How-
> ever, they can only be used by the corresponding
> class.
>> (Note: Used cards are discarded to the
>> shared "hangar.")
> 4. When a player's turn is over, play proceeds to the
>    next player.
> 5. When all players have had a turn, Phase One ends.
>    Play proceeds through additional phases until one
>    team achieves victory.

"Ah. I'm a novice at this game, myself. A nice, even contest," Dax said, nodding in satisfaction. "What matters is that there's more than one way of winning. You don't have to reach the goal if you can whittle down your opponents' life total. Although it will depend on circumstances to determine which strategy is more viable..."

The scoreboard floating over Dax's head began displaying more information for the players.

"I remember hearing something else about Mind Arena. This game has countless classes, leading to an almost infinite number of variant versions," Dax said.

Players started by choosing a class. It was the first decision they had to make in the game and would have a major impact on all that followed.

> **Class Choice**
> **You may choose from the following 4 classes.**
>> **Wizard:** +1 damage when using offensive magic.
>> **Healer:** +1 life restored when using healing magic.
>> **Traveler:** May add +1 square when using a dice
>> card (up to a maximum of 7 squares' movement).

**Trapper: Trap squares do not affect players with this class. In addition, trap squares they land on are strengthened.**

"This is the operator. This game is good for up to eight players, but for now we're going with a simple two-versus-two match."

"Good by me!" Dax said, shouting to be heard over an ear-splitting cheer. He stood with his arms folded. "For my partner, I've chosen another member of Tempest Cruiser."

A young woman with tan skin and light blue hair stepped up beside him. She looked calm and collected. "I shall be your second opponent. My name is Kelritch Shee. Officially, I'm Dax's subordinate. For some reason, we're frequently called the 'husband-and-wife comedy duo' or told to 'hurry up and get married,' but as far as I'm concerned Dax is merely a business partner. My feelings for him don't extend beyond that. I want to make sure we're clear on that point."

"Excellent, Kelritch. Are you ready?"

For a moment, she didn't say anything.

"What's the matter, Kelritch?"

"I thought I might get *some* reaction… I mean, ahem, never mind." She sighed and shook her head, although Fay wasn't quite sure why. "Please proceed, Dax."

"Very well. Fay!" Dax pointed squarely at Fay, his black coat whipping dramatically. "Now it's *your* turn! Choose your partner!"

Leshea, or Pearl? Fay turned. Standing there was one young woman with vermilion hair, smiling like she knew she was up to the challenge; and another young woman with golden hair who looked distinctly uncomfortable under the collective gaze of the spectators in the stadium.

"You look awfully nervous, Pearl," he said.

"Eeep! I mean, um! I'm...happy to sit this one out! It's two on two. You and Leshea would definitely be the stronger team!" Pearl waved her hands frantically to show that she didn't feel compelled to participate. "This is a big, important p-pride match between two branch offices! Just imagine if you picked me and we...we lost..."

"Say, Pearl." A slender finger tapped the golden-haired girl on the shoulder.

"Leshea?" She didn't even have to turn around, for Leshea had stepped up beside her, her vermilion hair billowing. Fay caught his breath at the sight, so beautiful and so assured was the smile on her face.

"You're not feeling *scared* of another *game*, are you?"

Pearl choked a little, a shudder passing through her. She understood what Leshea was saying. The memories were coming back. She'd hesitated to play before, afraid that, as with her rued defeat with Inferno, she would get everyone in trouble by screwing up. If she didn't step up now, it would show that she hadn't changed at all.

A light flickered to life in Pearl's eyes. "I am *not* scared! I refuse to be afraid of any more games!"

"So you think you can do this?" Leshea asked.

"I can and I will!"

"Attagirl." Leshea turned on her heel, and for a second—just a second—Fay could have sworn she'd winked at him. "I'll be right here, cheering you on. Fay, Pearl? Knock 'em dead."

"R-right!" Pearl said, clenching her fists. "Just you watch me, Leshea! I'm going to be the star of this game!"

At that, Dax started to smile. "Hoh. Fay could have teamed up with the Dragon God Leoleshea. A deity made flesh, said to achieve god-tier gameplay, literally. I was looking forward to seeing exactly what she could do...and he chooses you."

"I-I'll thank you not to underestimate me!" Pearl said, putting a hand to her chest and giving Dax her best glower. "All right, so maybe I'm not quite as good a player as Leshea, but I'm still a member of Fay's team—and I'm going to show you why!"

So the participants were chosen. Fay and Pearl versus Dax and Kelritch.

"This is the operator. You'll each be given a small communication device. You can use it to talk to your partner during the game."

"Wow! That's so neat!" Pearl said, looking awestruck as she was fitted with a tiny mic and a wireless earphone. "Testing, testing! Can you hear me, Fay?"

"Loud and clear. Nice to see they were thinking ahead. With a field this big, we'd give away all our strategies just talking normally or shouting."

They heard the operator's voice again. "Now you'll each be given five magic cards at random. You're allowed to tell your partner what you have, so feel free to use those comms devices."

"This is so neat, Fay! They show up right in front of us!" Pearl exclaimed, pointing. Five cards each were projected in front of Fay and Pearl.

Five magic cards. They were broadly divided into offensive, healing, and special magic. Each spell had a different effect. For example, "Mega Flame," one of the offensive cards in Pearl's hand, did two damage to a target player. All three types of cards might show up in your hand, but because they were dealt out randomly, you might have more of one type than the others.

"What a motley bunch of cards," Fay said, looking at his hand. "It figures." He was holding three healing cards, one offensive card...and one "Secret Spell" card that might just prove to be the linchpin of the game.

*But only the specified class can use a Secret Spell card,* Fay remembered. *That's a dilemma: Do I take the class that can use this card or not?*

The card in question was only for healers—but taking that class might be as good as admitting that he was holding this card.

"Tough decision, picking a class. What's in your hand, Pearl?" he asked.

"I don't have any Secret Spell cards," she said, obviously disappointed. Across from them, Dax and Kelritch were showing their cards to each other. "Oh! But I do have this High-Speed Magic one. That's pretty special." Pearl indicated the leftmost card in her hand. "I think it could be powerful, but it's tricky to use…"

"Hm? 'May be activated only when you have five or less life remaining and when this is the only card in your hand.' Geez, that is tough!"

The card Pearl was talking about fell under the special category. Since they each started with twenty life and five cards, she'd have to be in a pretty bad place to be able to make use of her High-Speed Magic card.

*But the trade-off is that it has a very interesting effect. Might make a good combo with my Secret Spell. Maybe we can work with this.*

So with that they took their cards into careful consideration while picking a class.

**Class Choice**
**You may choose from the following 4 classes.**
  **Wizard: +1 damage when using offensive magic.**
  **Healer: +1 life restored when using healing magic.**
  **Traveler: May add +1 square when using a dice card (up to a maximum of 7 squares' movement).**

**Trapper: Trap squares do not affect players with this class. In addition, trap squares they land on are strengthened.**

"Offhand, my take is that the Wizard and Healer classes are the simplest. They basically specialize in offense and healing, right? The Traveler and Trapper classes are more versatile. I'd sort of like to go with one of those... Interesting how they seem to be almost exact opposites."

"Huh?" Pearl said, not understanding. "I can see how the Wizard and Healer classes are opposites, but the Traveler and Trapper are, too?"

"Yeah. *Polar* opposites. The Traveler and the Healer form one 'group,' and the Trapper and the Wizard are another."

Pearl blinked, giving him a blank look. The Traveler and the Healer were some kind of group? And the Trapper and the Wizard were another? "Uh, Fay, maybe you could...explain what you mean?"

"It has to do with how they achieve victory. The Traveler tries to get to the goal as fast as possible. The Healer is all about preserving your life total. In other words, helping you last long enough to make it to the end. So they're both oriented around winning by reaching the goal."

"Oh! Y-yes, I see!"

"The Wizard and the Trapper are the other end of the spectrum," Fay said.

The Wizard was probably the more obvious of the two. It increased the damage dealt by magic cards. In other words, it was focused on reducing the opponents' life to zero before they could reach the finish line. The Trapper was similar. Notably, they could strengthen trap squares they landed on—naturally, with an eye toward dealing extra damage to the other team.

"Before we pick our classes, we should probably decide which way we want to approach the game."

"You mean if we want to try to reach the goal, we should pick Healer or Traveler, and if we want to take down the opponents, we should pick Wizard or Trapper, right?" Pearl said.

"You got it. Let's take another look at the cards in our hands."

It was obvious at a glance: they had far more healing magic than anything else. With so few offensive spells, reducing their opponents' life totals to zero would be a difficult strategy. No, they should go for the original sugoroku objective: reaching the goal.

*It would be pretty obvious. Basically, a frontal assault on the game. A Traveler and a Healer? Of course we're going for the finish line.* What interested Fay more was the young man in the black coat silently watching them. The incongruous look he was giving them was as eloquent as any speech. *He seems as confident as anything. And he doesn't try to hide it. I don't think he ever planned to just mosey to the goal line.*

Dax's plan was clear. Well, that helped Fay make his choice.

"I accept your challenge!" Fay said. He nodded at Dax and Kelritch, the two apostles from the Sacred Spring City of Mal-ra. "I choose the Traveler class!"

"A-and I choose Healer!" Pearl said.

"Ah," Dax said, nodding appreciatively. "So you guessed our plan. Time to compare answers, then. For my class, I choose Wizard!"

"And I also choose Wizard," said Kelritch.

Fay almost wasn't sure he'd heard right. "You *both* choose Wizard?"

But that was absurd! He could understand Dax taking that class, but he'd been assuming that Kelritch would pick Trapper. Having two different classes at your disposal gave you that many more options, a wider range of possible strategies. Instead, they'd chosen to confine themselves to focusing strictly on firepower.

*The Wizard class is all about pure damage-dealing. They've ruled out every other strategy—they're just going to try to decimate our life total!*

It was unvarnished aggression. A declaration that they would *not* allow Fay and Pearl to reach the goal.

"All players have chosen their classes. Get ready for game start!" the operator said, and things in the stadium immediately got more intense. Dice cards appeared in front of each of them, six cards simply numbered one, two, three, four, five, and six.

"So this is what they use instead of dice. Everyone picks a number—simultaneously."

Mind Arena was sugoroku without dice. Instead, you could choose any number you wanted from one to six and move forward that many spaces. Since the objective was, after all, to reach the finish line before your opponents, it might seem like you would want to pick six every time. But there was a catch...

"Aaahhh! I just realized something! Something unbelievable!" Pearl sounded almost crazed. She was pointing at the ground, at the huge board under their feet. It was possible to see what was on the squares ahead of them, just like on a real sugoroku board.

> **Square 1: Trap (serious damage if they landed here)**
> **Square 2: Gold (draw 2 cards)**
> **Square 3: Silver (draw 1 card)**
> **Square 4: Silver**
> **Square 5: Trap**
> **Square 6: Silver (this is the farthest they could move on the first turn)**
> **Square 7: Silver**

"Choosing six is the fastest way to the finish line, but if we both choose six at the same time, it would actually be *bad* for us!" Pearl said.

"Because we wouldn't be able to draw," Fay agreed. It was right there in the rules: if two or more people stopped on a silver or gold square at the same time, they couldn't draw cards.

*And this particular sugoroku variant is all about drawing cards on your way to the goal. That's why some of the smaller numbers can land you on gold squares.* Pick six and take a giant leap forward. But pick the humble two, and you would land on a golden square that would allow you to draw two magic cards. So: Advance substantially, or shore up your hand? The mind games started as soon as the real game did.

"Beginning Phase One. All players, please pick your dice card and place it facedown."

Even as the announcement echoed around the stadium, Fay was pointing at one of the cards. "Pearl, think about the classes we picked! We need to seize the initiative and keep it!"

"R-right!"

Their dice cards displayed facedown, as did those chosen by Dax and Kelritch.

The game began.

One by one, the dice cards the four of them had chosen flipped over. Fay and Dax had both picked six, Pearl four, and Kelritch two.

Fay and Dax had chosen the same number. Murmuring broke out in the crowd, but Dax nodded confidently. "I expected as much, Fay. I knew you wouldn't hesitate to take six. After all, the big numbers are the fastest way to the end."

"Great minds, huh?" Fay replied.

Turn order began with the person who had taken the largest number on the dice cards. *But if more than one person picks the same number, we go by whoever chose it first. There's a real-time element to the decisions in this game!*

That was why Fay had been quick to slap his card down before Dax could do the same.

"Two players have chosen the same number! By order of selection, Fay will take the first turn, followed by Dax."

"All right, here I go." Fay nodded at Pearl, then set off across the board. He moved six squares forward, arriving at the silver square. Normally he would have gotten a magic card out of it, but because Dax had chosen the same square, he couldn't draw.

He heard Dax behind him. "A question, Fay. Are you *sure* about that spot?"

"What do you mean?"

"Don't play dumb. Did you think I would forget that you picked the Traveler class?"

In other words, that he could add one square when he used his dice card. Fay, and Fay alone, could move seven spaces. The seventh space was also a silver square, meaning he could have gone there and gotten a card.

But without missing a beat Fay said, "I'm not using my Traveler ability."

"Clearly. You wanted to land on the same square as me to rob me of my draw." The corners of his mouth drew up in a smile; he was patently enjoying himself. "You should continue your turn, Fay."

"Don't have to tell me twice."

He'd stopped on the sixth square of the sugoroku board that filled the huge stadium. He couldn't draw—but he could still decide whether to use any of the five magic cards in his hand.

"Hey, Operator," Fay said. "This is a two-on-two battle, right?

Pearl and I stand or fall together—if one of us reaches the goal, we both win. If one of us reaches zero life, we both lose. So what about our cards? Can we trade the magic cards in our hand?"

"Not allowed," replied Kelritch, from where she was patiently waiting for her turn. "The rules define each player's hand as belonging to them. Some magic cards, however, can *effectively* allow you to swap cards. If you draw one of them, then feel free."

"Okay. Just curious." Fay nodded, appearing to think for just a second. It was unlikely that any of the spectators noticed the way he ever so briefly met Pearl's eyes and nodded, the smallest of gestures. "In that case, I end my turn. I won't use a magic card."

"It's my turn, then!" Dax said. His six got him to the silver square, but with Fay there, he couldn't draw a card. But whereas Fay had simply finished his turn at that point, Dax bellowed, "You chose to conserve your hand, Fay. Well, I choose the opposite! On this turn, I use a Wizard's Secret Spell!"

"What, already?!" Fay burst out.

Secret Spells were the most powerful among the many cards. It was Dax's good luck that he had drawn a Wizard's Secret Spell in his opening hand. But he was going to take that potentially game-changing card and use it...on his first turn?

"Behold! I cast the barrier spell, Burning Rhythm!"

The AR image added a field of flames all around the playing area.

**Burning Rhythm: When any damage occurs, suffer 1 additional damage.**

That was all. Pearl seemed a bit caught off guard—she'd probably been assuming that a Wizard's Secret Spell would inflict tons of damage at a stroke. She'd been expecting more than this.

"U-um," she said, raising her hand. "I just want to make sure of something. The extra damage from this Burning Rhythm card...it only applies to us, right?"

"No," Dax said brusquely.

"Sorry?"

"This card affects all players. If I were to be attacked, for example, I would also sustain additional damage. A double-edged sword if there ever was one."

"What? B-but why would you do that?!" Pearl's mouth hung agape; she was completely confused. If choosing Wizard represented a plan to win by annihilating the enemy, why would he use a card that could even damage him?

"I conclude my turn," Dax said.

"O-okay! It's my turn next, then!" Pearl said, curling her fingers into a fist. She proceeded four squares forward, in accordance with the dice card she'd picked, where she landed on a silver square and drew a magic card. Now she had six in her hand. "I'm also going to conserve my cards! Turn over!"

"So we come to the last. Myself," Kelritch said. There was murmuring from the crowd, all eyes focused on Dax's partner. "I draw two cards," she said. Kelritch had chosen two on the dice— the gold square.

*So I'm a Traveler and Pearl's a Healer. Both classes are oriented toward getting to the goal*, Fay thought. Which led to one conclusion: they had to go for large numbers every time. Fay had chosen six on the dice, and Pearl four. Her reasoning had been that Dax would know Fay would choose six, and she thought Dax might choose four to fake him out. (Five would land on a trap square, so no one would choose it.) But that thinking had betrayed her.

*Kelritch isn't thinking about what we're doing at all. She went straight for the gold square to get the most possible cards!*

Kelritch now had the biggest hand with seven cards. The Wizard class added damage, and she was obviously hoping to expand her repertoire of offensive options in order to smash through their life total.

"Have a look at this." With a flourish of her hand she pointed at one of the seven cards that floated in front of her. "This time you'll see *real* offensive magic. I cast Twin Bolt. Fay, Pearl, you each take one damage."

"Oh... Just one? Phew," Pearl said with evident relief. After all, they each had twenty life. One damage was practically nothing.

"No, it's worse than that," Fay said.

"Wha?"

"I see what they're up to. Pearl, this could be bad. That Burning Rhythm card is nothing to sneeze at." Fay felt sweat trickling down his cheek, but he had nothing to wipe it away with. He looked at the board over their heads.

Fay takes 4 damage. Remaining life: 16.
Pearl takes 4 damage. Remaining life: 16.

"Whaaat?! I don't get it! The card only deals one point of damage!" Pearl was waving her hands frantically. "Their math must be wrong!"

"Calm down, Pearl. They've got the math right. When a Wizard does damage, they deal one *additional* damage. Then there's another additional point of damage from Burning Rhythm."

"O-okay... But that should only be three damage..."

"No, it's four. *Burning Rhythm activated twice.* Once when we took the attack damage, and once when we took the additional damage from the Wizard bonus."

So this was how it worked out:

1. They took 1 damage from Twin Bolt.
2. Kelritch's Wizard class ability activated, inflicting 1 additional damage. (Total: 2)
3. Burning Rhythm was triggered by the damage from step 1, inflicting 1 additional damage. (Total: 3)
4. Burning Rhythm was triggered a second time by the damage from step 2, inflicting 1 additional damage. (Total: 4)

That Secret Spell was turning out to be a key play, spewing additional damage left, right, and center. Normally, Twin Bolt would have done no more than two damage even with Burning Rhythm in play. Combined with the Wizard ability, however, it ballooned to a staggering eight damage between the two of them.

"And the effect is continuous. This is going to get worse."

"Are we going to keep taking these huge hits to our life total?!"

The moment the damage to Fay and Pearl was displayed, the stadium erupted, practically vibrating with cheers. A chant of "Dax! Dax! Dax!" sounded like it would bring the place down.

"Y-y-yikes! So this is what it's like to be the away team... Is there *anyone* out there cheering for us?!"

"Good question..."

The chief secretary had called Dax Mal-ra's foremost apostle. The city's hero was fighting, carrying the pride of his hometown on his shoulders. Fay wasn't surprised that he and Pearl found themselves without any port in this storm.

*So we take damage, Dax's team gains the advantage, and the crowd goes wild.* Could have seen that one coming.

"Just ignore them. If you're enjoying the game, nothing else matters, right?" he said. He was talking as much to himself as to Pearl. They had to focus on the game.

That was when he heard a voice from behind him. "Y-you can do it, Master Fay!" A dark-haired young woman was clenching

her fists and shouting from the front row of the spectator seating.
It was Nel Reckless. The last they'd seen of her, she'd been running down the staff corridor, but now she was cheering them on
at the top of her lungs.

"Nel?"

"I told you I'd be rooting for you! I can't out-cheer this entire
crowd, but I can at least be here to watch you fight!"

"Huh! I think I'm starting to get it."

"G-get what, Master Fay?"

"That you might be a bit of a strange one, but you've got a
good heart. Thanks." He gave her a little smile and a wave.

In his mind, he was only expressing his gratitude. But then
they heard "Ohh!"

"Hey! Nel?!" Fay exclaimed. She'd put her hand to her heart,
gripped the railing of the stands, and swooned. "Hrn... I'm s-sorry,
Master Fay. I was undone by your unexpected profession of love..."

"When did I profess anything like that?!"

"Hmph..." Leshea was sitting with her arms crossed in the
seat beside Nel— When had she gotten there? She was watching
them both, and her eyes were very, very cold. Fay could almost
feel her gaze physically crushing them into the ground. "Fay?"
she said.

"Y-yeah, Leshea?"

"*I* will be doing plenty of cheering for you, so try to focus on
the game, all right?"

"Yeah, sure..."

Leshea gave him a carefully crafted smile. This was clearly
not the moment for any attempt to discuss things with her, much
less argue. Her eyes were still boring a hole in his back when Fay
turned around to face Dax again.

"All right, Pearl, let's concentrate. By which I mean...ignore
the murderous intent coming from behind us."

"R-right! But, um, Fay... What about our life total?" Pearl sounded uneasy. It was understandable—after all, a single play by the opponents had cost them twenty percent of their life. "I know we've still got plenty left. But doesn't this mean we're basically starting the game at a huge disadvantage?"

"This isn't the start," Fay said.

"Huh?"

"I'm afraid we may already be in the mid-game. With that sort of firepower, they have every chance of wiping us both out."

"If you think that's encouraging, it's not!"

"I expected them to bring the pain, but this is more than I even anticipated. Drawing that Wizard's Secret Spell right off the bat really helped them hit the ground running."

The sugoroku board on which they stood occupied the entire arena within the stadium. Fay peered as far into the distance as he could.

"I've got thirty-eight squares to go to the goal, and you've got forty, Pearl. Which means even if we move six squares each turn, we'd still need about seven turns to get there."

The enemy had specialized in firepower, while Fay's and Pearl's classes were designed specifically to throw a wrench into the brawlers' play style. *Pearl's a Healer. If she can restore enough health, we might survive—at least for a while. As a Traveler, I can cover the board faster than anyone.* So what if the Traveler were to try to go as fast as possible, with the Healer keeping him alive along the way?

"You really think you can do it?" asked Kelritch softly. The tan young woman seemed to see right through them. "My turn isn't over. I cast a barrier: Chains of Malice."

**Chains of Malice: Whenever a player uses a card, they take 1 damage.**

"A-another barrier spell?! Why don't they just attack us directly with their magic?!" Pearl said, her eyes wide. A Wizard ability, after all, was to do additional damage when inflicting magic damage on opponents. As Kelritch had just demonstrated, when combined with Burning Rhythm, it could add up fast. And yet she'd chosen to lay down another barrier instead. If anything, that made Fay and Pearl even more worried about what was going on.

"You'll see very soon," Kelritch said calmly. "I end my turn with five cards left in my hand."

"So much for Phase One. We've each got a sense of the other's strategy now," Dax said, smiling confidently. "Your objective, Fay, is to reach the finish line as fast as possible. Whereas Kelritch and I will be piling on all our firepower to shatter you long before you get anywhere near it!"

So the first phase concluded.

Fay: 16 life, 5 cards, currently on square 6 (38 squares to the goal)

Pearl: 16 life, 6 cards, currently on square 4

Dax: 20 life, 4 cards, currently on square 6

Kelritch: 20 life, 5 cards, currently on square 2

*That's an eight-point difference in total life*, Fay thought. *But Pearl and I have eleven cards between us, while they just have nine. Maybe we can use that to our advantage.*

He'd managed to conserve his hand in a game where more cards meant more options. And since he hadn't used any cards yet, his opponents still couldn't be completely sure of what his strategy might be.

*There's not all that much luck involved in this game. Strategy is the deciding factor. And whether or not your strategy is working reveals itself in the difference in life totals.*

All right, so what made a strategy better or worse? The answer was *reading*. Who did a better job of deducing their opponents' methods based on the number of cards they were holding and the proverbial pips on the dice? Which player would come up with the most effective counterstrategy? That was the real question.

*I can't let them figure it out. Can't let them guess that Pearl and I have only had one aim from the very start.*

They only had one strategy. From the moment they'd picked Traveler and Healer for their classes, they'd been committed.

"Pearl," Fay had said softly to the young woman standing beside him. "There's one technique, one killer play, that works in every card game. You know what it is?"

"Er? N-no, what?"

"*Don't empty your hand.* Make sure you're always holding *something*, even if it's a useless card. It gives you room to bluff."

Always, as it were, keep an ace up your sleeve. No matter how dire the situation, that final card could turn out to be the one you need to turn everything around and snatch an upset victory. That, at least, was what you wanted your opponent thinking— but they wouldn't be thinking that if you didn't have anything left in your hand.

"The corollary to that is don't hesitate to use anything that *isn't* the last card in your hand. If we try to save them up, those two Wizards will obliterate us."

"Right! That makes sense!"

The game entered Phase Two.

First, everyone picked their dice cards again. At the moment, Kelritch stood on the second square, Pearl on the fourth, while Fay and Dax together occupied square six.

**Square 8: Gold square (the farthest Kelritch could move)**
**Square 9: Silver square**
**Square 10: Silver (the farthest Pearl could move)**
**Square 11: Trap**
**Square 12: Silver (the farthest Fay and Dax could move)**

"Begin Phase Two. Choose your dice cards."

"Pearl!" Fay shouted. "Don't hesitate. *Use 'em!*"
"Right!"

The players' dice cards revealed themselves, and there was an audible reaction from the crowd when they saw the numbers. In order of selection, they were:

Dax: six, Kelritch: six, Fay: six, Pearl: four.

Fay and Dax would wind up together on a silver square again. The numbers that really drew amazement, though, were those last two. Pearl had chosen four in the first round, and again now. Kelritch had gone for two before, but now selected six. In other words, Pearl and Kelritch would wind up on the gold square together. And it wasn't a coincidence. It was clear that they'd deliberately sought to undermine each other.

The tan girl's eyebrow twitched, the first ripple in an expression that had been as still as a calm pool. "You're actually coming for me, aren't you?" she said. "You realized I was trying to land on as many gold squares as I could and contrived to land on the same square as me so I couldn't get more cards."

"W-well, of course I did!" Pearl glared back at Kelritch. "A Wizard's firepower is what makes them scary, but you can't use any magic if you don't have any cards. Naturally, I saw that you would want to go for the gold squares!"

Pearl and Kelritch stood on the gold eighth square. Fay and Dax, meanwhile, stood on the twelfth square, a silver one. Since each of them had ended up on the same square as another player, nobody got to draw any cards. If that kept happening and they kept using the cards in their hands, eventually they wouldn't have any left. That would play right into Fay and Pearl's hands, since all they wanted was to get to the end.

"Very well. This calls for a change in strategy. I declare to you that starting on my next turn, I will not try to land on any more gold squares," Kelritch said.

"What?!" Pearl said.

"Still think you can guess where I'm going next? If you can't land yourself on the same square as me, you won't be able to stop me from getting those cards."

Pearl gritted her teeth. "Y-your little mind games won't work on me!" She raised one hand, talking as much to herself as to Kelritch. "I'm going on the attack! High-Speed Magic: Pearl Fire!"

Pearl Fire? Fay, Dax, and Kelritch—along with everyone in the audience—looked puzzled. They were all wondering the same thing: Was there such a card?

"Uh, Pearl—," Fay started, but she interrupted him.

"High-Speed Magic has the advantage of being usable at any time! Even during your opponent's turn. That makes it perfect for a sneak attack!"

"Yeah, I know. What I *don't* know is—"

As Fay spoke, the card Pearl had pointed at flipped itself over. It was Mega Flame. *Deal two damage to target player.*

"That's not the card you said it was!" Fay said.

"Yes, it is, Fay! Pearl Fire. Mega Flame is a dumb name, and I could never be happy using it!"

"I don't think it's so much about whether you feel cool or whatever. You're confusing everyone, including me!"

"So, there you have it: Pearl Fire!"

A three-dimensional flame spewed forth, doing three damage to Dax.

"Heh! How about that, Fay? Mega Flame normally only does two damage, but with a great name like Pearl Fire, it hits harder!"

"That's just the added damage from Burning Rhythm. And Pearl, uh, I'm sure you realize this, but you'll take two damage, too."

"What?" At that moment, sparks exploded in front of her face. "Eeek! Wh-why is it doing that?!"

The barrier spell, Chains of Malice, had activated. It was triggered by the use of a card and did one damage to Pearl. Then, triggered by that damage, Burning Rhythm did an additional point of damage.

"Wh-what do we do, Fay?! I was trying to preserve my life, but instead I ended up losing two points!"

"You forgot, huh?"

There were two barrier spells active, Chains of Malice and Burning Rhythm. As long as they were in effect, every card played would do two damage to the user. If Fay and Pearl tried to push back against the Wizards and their power, they would only hasten their own demise.

"Interesting. So if using a card does two damage, then if we heal two life, we'd essentially even out to zero. If we used a card that only healed one life, we'd actually come out worse."

Pearl gasped. "They've countered my Healer abilities!"

"Do you have any barriers, Pearl? Like, you know, something that restores life every time you draw a card or something?"

Pearl gritted her teeth again. "No... I didn't draw anything like that. What about you, Fay?"

"Me neither." Fay had five cards in his hand: three healing cards he could, in principle, use immediately, and two "dead" cards he couldn't activate now.

*So neither of us drew any barrier spells. Too bad. I would have liked to be able to get rid of at least one of their barriers...*

Burning Rhythm was particularly nefarious. It could throw off all their strategies, all their calculations. Well, that was what made it a Wizard's Secret Spell.

"I believe it's our turn," Kelritch said, her gaze more piercing than ever. "Notwithstanding your rude interruption with your High-Speed Magic, Pearl, turn order will now proceed according to the numbers on the dice cards."

Specifically, they would go from largest number to smallest, with ties being resolved in favor of the person who chose the card first. (This added an element of real-time strategy.) This made the turn order: Dax (six), Kelritch (six), Fay (six), and Pearl (four).

"Looks like I have the initiative!" Dax said. He moved six spaces forward, to land on the twelfth space. Then he pointed to one of the cards in his hand. "Pearl, is it? Time to take an eye for an eye. I cast Dax Thunder!"

*Dax Thunder?* Another card name nobody recognized. Fay and Pearl, of course, but even the spectators looked confused.

There was a long pause before Dax's partner, Kelritch, said in a wilting voice, "He means Blizzard. That's the proper name of the card." She was blushing. "I'm sure he's just...pushing back against 'Pearl Fire.' Dax does hate to lose..."

"So, Pearl." Dax turned his intense stare on the blond girl. "I must say, I'm impressed. To have the audacity to give cards your own names when you're playing Mind Arena for the very first time. A notion wild enough to be worthy of praise."

"That's what I'm talking about!" Pearl said.

"Then let me match like for like. I dub this card Dax Thunder!"

"Wait, he's competing with her? And where did he get the

'thunder' thing, anyway?" Fay mumbled, but it was lost in the roar of the stadium.

Dax Thunder (that is, Blizzard) did three damage, plus Dax's Wizard ability, plus the additional damage from Burning Rhythm. In all, it took six points out of Pearl's life total of fourteen.

"I'm down to eight life already! And we're only on the second turn! By the next turn, or maybe the one after that, my back's really going to be against the wall!"

"The next turn? No. I intend to finish this here," Kelritch said, and then she was moving, advancing her six spaces to the gold square. "It's my turn. I cast Crash of the Heavens and this card specifically requires that I take one damage to play the card—boosted to four damage by Rhythm and Chain—in order to do four damage to a target opponent. Combined with my Wizard ability and Burning Rhythm, that's seven total damage. Pearl, you have one life remaining."

"I—I have High-Speed Magic I can use!" Pearl cried. "I cast a healing spell, Hope in Abundance! I remove one card in my hand from the game to play it, and in exchange I can reduce damage done to me up to two times the number of cards in my hand before I removed that card. That means I can nullify up to eight damage, and combined with my Healer ability, that makes it nine..."

"You fell for it," Dax said.

"Huh?"

"I cast my own High-Speed Magic: the Price of Greed." His words were terrible to hear. "It can only be played when an opponent uses healing magic. That healing spell is canceled!"

Pearl gasped.

"I deliberately provoked you into using a card," Kelritch said. "Your magic is as good as wasted, and my seven damage remains,

reducing your life total to one. Further, your use of Hope in Abundance activates Chains of Malice. There goes your one life. You're down to zero." And that meant she was out. "Or do you have another High-Speed Magic spell among those three cards you have left?"

"W-well, I..."

"If not, then this is over," Kelritch said, like a judge pronouncing a guilty verdict. "Chains of Malice and Rhythm do two damage, reducing Pearl's life total to nothing and—"

"Hey, don't worry," Fay said. He pointed to a card in his own hand—one that would reverse that verdict. "Just 'cause Pearl doesn't have any spells left, doesn't mean I don't. I cast the High-Speed Magic Bandaged Heart. Reduce damage to a player by two!"

"You think you can stop me?!"

"Wouldn't be much fun if the game ended so soon, would it?"

Pearl was back from the cusp—but she was down to one life.

*They're focusing their fire. But I expected that going in. It only makes sense that they would single out Pearl. It's a pain, but I'd do the same thing in their shoes.*

There were two ways to win Mind Arena: one team member had to get to the goal...or *one* of the opponents had to be reduced to zero life. So they didn't have to worry about Fay; they could just focus on bringing down Pearl.

"Don't forget that in *this* arena, helping your friend means hurting yourself!" Dax crowed, pointing at Fay. "You used a card, which activates Chains of Malice. Burning Rhythm adds to that. That's two damage for you! You're at fourteen life!"

"Yeah. Which is exactly what I wanted." Now it was Fay's turn. He moved forward six spaces, bringing him level with Dax. "I use the damage I just took as the trigger to cast Swords of the Heavenly Host!"

This card could only be used during phases in which you had sustained damage, but it did five damage to one opponent.

"That's six damage for you, Dax!"

"I can't believe this!" Kelritch gawked. "You even factored *that* into your use of that healing magic?!"

Indeed he had. Swords of the Heavenly Host had been one of the dead cards in Fay's hand. It was a powerful spell, but he could only use it when he'd taken damage—and Dax and Kelritch had only been going after Pearl. With them refusing to attack him, Fay was stuck with the card in his hand.

"Swords of the Heavenly Host is normally a way of striking back when you've been attacked. I never thought of using the supplementary damage from Chains of Rage to trigger it... I assumed you would be completely focused on healing your friend!" Kelritch hissed. Then she said, "So, Fay, is that the end of your turn?"

"Not quite. I'm also going to cast a Self-Applied Magic spell, Soul's Sacrifice. I discard one card from my hand. That card and Soul's Sacrifice both go in the hangar, and Pearl and I each gain three life."

If they were going to focus their fire on Pearl, then the solution was simple: Fay would focus his healing on her, too. Once his turn was over, Pearl would have a turn when she could continue healing herself.

"It's my turn!" Pearl said. She moved four spaces forward, landing on the gold square beside Kelritch. There were three cards in her hand. She was out of High-Speed Magic cards, but that simply meant her remaining spells were all things she could use now on her turn. "I cast Oasis to restore four life. Plus, my Healer's bonus makes it five! And I use two of them!"

At the same time, however, each of her cards triggered Chains of Malice and Burning Rhythm. Ultimately, she recouped six life.

"That's the end of my turn!"

So at the end of Phase Two, they stood:
Fay: 13 life, 1 card, currently on square 12 (32 squares
to the goal)
Pearl: 10 life, 1 card, currently on square 8
Dax: 7 life, 2 cards, currently on square 12
Kelritch: 16 life, 4 cards, currently on square 8

They'd survived—and they'd even managed to get closer to
the finish line. *But our situation is definitely worse. I'm particularly worried that now they're the ones holding most of the cards.*
Dax's low life total might be comforting at a glance, but he and
Kelritch held six cards between them while Fay and Pearl had
only two. *Dax's life total is a distraction. I can almost guarantee
he has some healing cards in his hand. For practical purposes, I
should assume his life is at least ten—maybe even thirteen.*
In other words, when everything was accounted for, the difference between the two teams was stark. Fay's opponents could
have two or three major spells left in their hands. Whereas Pearl's
life total could be wiped out in the next round.

"It looks like you understand the position you're in. We're
holding all the cards here—literally." Dax grinned. "You can give
up any fantasies of reaching the finish line, Fay. Phase Three is
when *we* seize the victory!"

Currently, Pearl and Kelritch were on square eight, while Fay
and Dax stood on square twelve.

**Square 13: Silver square**
**Square 14: Gold square (the farthest Pearl and Kelritch**
**could move)**
**Square 15: Silver**

**Square 16: Trap**
**Square 17: Silver**
**Square 18: Silver (the farthest Fay and Dax could move)**
**Square 19: Gold**

"Proceeding to Phase Three. Players, choose your dice cards."

"Pearl!" Fay shouted, turning to his partner. "We need to stay focused on our strategy! Right to the bitter end!"

"I sure will!"

The dice cards flipped over.

Pearl: six, Fay: six, Kelritch: five, and...Dax: four.

A buzz swept through the audience. It was clear that Dax was playing at something. Were people so startled because he'd finally chosen something other than a six? That was part of it...

"No way!" Pearl said, looking at Dax's dice card as if she couldn't believe what she was seeing. Fay was thunderstruck, too—but he'd had a sense that Dax might try something aggressive like this.

*He's laying all his cards on the table, so to speak. He really does mean to finish it this turn!*

"What do you think you're doing?!" Pearl said, a big bead of sweat rolling down her cheek. Her eyes were fixed on Dax, who stood with his arms crossed. Triumphant. Terrifying. "Four squares ahead of you is a trap! Why would you go there on purpose and take damage?!"

Fay was going to land on square eighteen, which was silver. Pearl was headed for the fourteenth square, a gold one. And Kelritch was going to land on another silver square, square thirteen. Dax, though, was headed for square sixteen—a trap.

"You'll see soon enough." He returned Pearl's gaze, his look piercing. "But you've got the biggest number on the dice cards. Go ahead. Take your turn."

"A-all right, I will!" Pearl strode across the sugoroku board. Just for a second, she could be seen stealing a glance back at Kelritch. She was worried—she didn't know what the blue-haired girl was thinking. Gold squares were the best for adding more cards to your hand, so Pearl had assumed Kelritch would also choose six. The better to thwart Pearl. But the other girl seemed to have seen straight through her.

The only thing that worried her more was Dax, who stood behind her.

"I land on a gold square and draw two cards. I use one of them: the Super Spell, Pearl Barrier!"

As one, the entire stadium had a single thought: *Not again.*

"Pearl... Just making sure, but that's not its real name, is it?" Fay said.

"I guess it's actually called Curtain of Darkness. It neutralizes the next magic spell that targets me! And with that, I end my turn!"

"What's the use of confusing your own partner?" Fay said. But then he added, "Eh, it's all good. My turn next!"

He moved up to a silver square—and for the first time, he decided to activate his Traveler power. "I'm going to use my ability as a Traveler to add one square to my dice card. That means I can move seven spaces." And the seventh space was gold. Just like Pearl, he drew two cards, bringing him up to three in his hand.

"My turn's over," he said.

"Saving your cards? Hoping to protect yourself against us?" said Kelritch. She was next in the turn order. "That was a good choice with your magic, Pearl. You knew Dax and I had deliberately chosen to move late, and you were worried about what we might be planning. But that barrier won't be enough to save you."

Kelritch walked across the board, her footsteps clicking as she went. She stopped on a silver square and drew one card.

"It doesn't matter how careful you are. Our victory is assured." She pointed at one of her cards with a delicate finger. "I cast Mega Flame."

"No! You're using Pearl Fire?!"

"No. I'm using Mega Flame." (Pearl's interjection proved altogether fruitless.) "I target Pearl, of course."

"I th-thought you might! But you're forgetting about my barrier!"

"Curtain of Darkness? Not at all. I've accounted for that."

The two spells canceled each other out, but Kelritch wasn't even watching the projection. She was already looking at her hand. "I hold four cards. I cast Absolute Resource Equality. All players must draw—or *discard*—until they have four cards in their hand."

"Wha?! Wh-what are you planning?!" Pearl choked.

"Go ahead and draw. I'm not worried. For my last play on this turn, I'm going to set this timed spell." One of the cards from Kelritch's hand floated to the center of the playing field, still facedown.

**Timed Spell: ???**
**Reveals and activates at end of phase. Effect unknown.**

They might not know what it was going to do, but one thing they could be sure of: Kelritch had as much as declared that she had set a trap for them. They had the remainder of this phase to prepare themselves—but that only implied that the spell would do something very powerful.

*Kelritch seems really confident about this. Is it a spell that's going to wipe out the last of our life?*

At that moment, Kelritch added calmly: "Pearl."

"Y-yes?! What?"

"That spell I used, Absolute Resource Equality. Dax and I drew a total of three cards between us, as did you and your partner, so you might think nothing has changed. But you would be wrong about that. As you'll soon see."

Three of their turns were already over, leaving only...

"My turn." Dax raced forward, his coat flapping behind him. He was headed straight for the red trap square. "I don't get to draw any cards, and I take substantial damage. You might think there's no advantage to this square, right?" The tall, slim young man turned. "Players in Mind Arena choose the number of squares they move. That means they can choose to avoid traps—and there's a proportionate penalty when they don't."

Yet his tone was unmistakably one of victory.

"I have seven life, and this trap does seven damage. That would mean I lose—*if* the trap does its damage to me. But by using the High-Speed Magic spell Double Trap, I can change the target of the damage!"

"What?!" Pearl cried, her mouth hanging open.

Beside her, Fay was gritting his teeth. "I figured you must have had something like that up your sleeve! Why else would you deliberately land on a trap square? You'd have to have some way to deflect or redirect the damage."

"Yes. And if you'll recall the rules, Fay, *damage from traps may not be reduced.*"

Fay caught his breath.

"Ah, so you see. The damage transferred by Double Trap can't be reduced. Pearl's life total is eight, and this trap does seven damage—which, with the effect of Burning Rhythm, becomes eight!"

"So that's what that Mega Flame was about!"

Damage from traps couldn't be reduced, but the effect *could* be neutralized. Pearl's Curtain of Darkness could have protected her from it. Kelritch had used her Mega Flame to consume Pearl's barrier. Perfect partner play.

"This is over!" Dax shouted.

"No! It's not!" Fay yelled back. "Don't forget, I've got a healthy four cards in my hand now. I cast the High-Speed spell A Twin's Agony. I can voluntarily redirect damage taken by Pearl to me!"

The damage couldn't be reduced. But it *could* be redirected, just as Dax had done.

"Pearl takes three damage, and I take five!" Fay said.

"So you had the right card for the moment. Very interesting." The conviction in Dax's eyes never wavered. Never mind that Fay's interference had robbed him of the chance to finish off Pearl. "I've been waiting for *you* to use a card, Fay."

"Say what?"

"I cast the High-Speed spell Gag Order! Until the end of this phase, you can't use cards of any kind!"

*He's preventing me from using cards?! Sounds like I had to use a card to trigger that effect. But why now?*

> Fay: 6 life, 3 cards, currently on square 19 (Gold)
> Pearl: 5 life, 4 cards, currently on square 14 (Gold)
> Dax: 3 life, 2 cards, currently on square 16 (Trap)
> Kelritch: 10 life, 3 cards, currently on square 13 (Silver)

"Fay—your cards!"

"Keep a cool head, Pearl. Maybe I can't do anything, but his spell doesn't affect your cards. Anyway, Phase Three is already over!"

Dax, the last player in the round, ended his turn. What good had it done him to prevent Fay from using cards for the rest of the round when the round was over?

"Oh, it's not over," Kelritch said. "With your cards in stasis, Fay, you can't save Pearl anymore."

"What?"

"All players have finished their turns, so the phase concludes. Which means my timed spell reveals itself!"

The facedown card flipped over, and when they saw what it was, Fay and Pearl froze in horror.

> **Timed Magic Spell: Destiny**
> 1. At the conclusion of the phase, all players take damage equal to the number of cards they drew this phase.
> 2. If a player drew 4 or more cards, they take 10 damage.

*So that's what this was all about! That's why Dax deliberately landed on the trap, and why Kelritch avoided the gold square!* Anticipating Kelritch's ambush, they had tried to draw as few cards as possible.

Fay had drawn three cards (he'd landed on a gold square, then drawn one with Absolute Resource Equality). Dax had taken two (both from Absolute Resource Equality), as had Kelritch (a silver square plus one from Absolute Resource Equality).

And then there was Pearl.

"No... No!" The blood had drained from the blond girl's face. She'd drawn four cards.

"I see you've connected the dots. You've figured out the real reason we let you draw those cards. It was all in preparation for this."

Flames began to well up from the Destiny card.

"You have five life left, Pearl, and this spell is going to do ten damage. Think you've got enough in your Healer's bag of tricks to save yourself?"

Pearl bit her lip. Her silence was her answer.

"I thought not. Clearly, using the card-prevention spell on *him* was the right choice."

The Destiny card shone brighter; ten lethal damage ready to inflict itself on Pearl.

"I...I refuse to be a burden to Fay and Leshea! This phase isn't over yet! I won't let it be!" Pearl yelled. She pointed to a card in her hand, the second from the right. "I cast Last Stand! It can only be used when your life total would otherwise be zero!"

**High-Speed Magic: Last Stand**
**Gain another turn. When that turn is over, you take 20 damage.**

Dax reeled back. "Wha—?!"

"But that—!" Kelritch, too, looked thrown off.

Destiny was a timed spell; its effect activated at the end of a phase. However, Pearl's additional turn would take place before the end of the phase—thereby delaying the onset of the timed spell.

"But the more powerful the card, the greater the price. If I can't win by the end of this turn, I'll take twenty damage from Last Stand and lose."

"A dirty little trick!" the tan girl said, glaring at Pearl. "Your partner Fay can't use his cards. Are you suggesting you can bring our life total to zero all by yourself?"

Pearl looked straight at her, her jaw set. "I'm not afraid to lose. The only thing I'm afraid of is letting this end when I still haven't learned to stop running from games! If I run away now, it'll mean nothing's changed!"

Last Stand activated, and Pearl Diamond prepared to take one last turn. A turn on which she was gambling all her life.

**Game: Mind Arena**
**Win Condition 1: On her final turn, Pearl reaches the goal line.**
**Win Condition 2: On her final turn, Pearl reduces Dax or Kelritch to 0 life.**
**Lose Condition: Pearl fails to fulfill either of these Win Conditions.**
**At the end of the turn, Last Stand will deal a penalty of 20 damage to Pearl, and she will be out of the game. (Note: Pearl will lose *before* the timed spell Destiny activates.)**

*We've got two ways to win this. But there's still thirty squares to the goal. No way you could get that far in a single turn.*

At least that made the plan obvious: Pearl would have to take Dax or Kelritch down to zero life. She clenched her fist. The stadium roared, but Fay was watching the young woman who was his partner.

*I've passed the baton. Now all I can do is trust the partner I picked.*

One last turn. One more chance to put everything on the line: their life total, their cards, their strategy.

"It's my turn!" Pearl said, grabbing the five dice card. That would put her on the same gold square as Fay, the nineteenth space on the board. She got to draw two cards. Now Pearl had three life and five cards in her hand.

"First I'm going to play Life Pulse. It normally heals four life, but if your remaining life total is three or less, it heals nine instead!" After factoring in her Healer's bonus, Chains of Malice, and Burning Rhythm, Pearl had eleven life. Enough to survive using all four cards in her hand.

"Trust yourself, Pearl! This is the turn to use everything you've got!"

"I will, Fay! I have three offensive cards in my hand. My target, of course, will be you with your three life!" she said, pointing at the young man in the black coat. "For my first trick, Counterbolt! It does four base damage, plus Burning Rhythm makes five. With that—"

"The perfect time for my High-Speed spell, First Aid. I reduce the damage taken by five."

Dax was down to one life.

"I'm not out of spells yet!" said Pearl. Two of the remaining three cards in her hand were offensive magic. "If this next Pearl Fire reaches you, you're toast!"

"Are you forgetting about me?" Kelritch brushed the blue hair from her forehead and moved to defend her partner. "I use the High-Speed spell Saint's Charity to heal four life. And I use a second to heal myself. Dax's life total is two; mine is ten."

Pearl gasped.

"Those were the two healing cards in my hand. So close, but so far, Pearl."

"Not at all," Pearl said with a shake of her head. "I figured at least one of you must be holding a healing card or two. That's why I've been saving *this* spell until you used them up!" She pointed at a card, which flipped itself over. It was an offensive spell, Ancient Word. It dealt damage equal to the total number of damage-dealing offense spells used this phase. "The spells cast this phase included Mega Flame, Double Trap, Destiny, Counterbolt, and

Pearl Fire—five cards! With Burning Rhythm, that comes to six damage! That means we win, Dax!"

Dax had two life left and one card in his hand—but he couldn't use that card because emptying his hand would cause two damage to him. He had no way to defend himself against Ancient Word.

"So it would seem." To Pearl's amazement, her opponent simply crossed his arms and closed his eyes.

"H-how can you look so calm about it?!"

"That was brilliant gameplay," Dax said without opening his eyes. His whisper carried all the way through the stadium, which had gone silent. "Your partner, Fay, unable to act. And you, alone, put Kelritch's and my backs up against the wall. I would never have imagined. You are certainly no burden to Fay."

"A-are you admitting you lost?!"

"I'm one step ahead."

The last card in Dax's hand floated up. "I activate the High-Speed spell Karmic Cycle! All damage taken by me is redirected to my partner! Including the damage taken from emptying my hand!"

"What?!"

"Kelritch has ten life, and my total damage is only eight. Hence, we both survive."

Dax with two life left, and Kelritch the same. They had shared their resources to the utmost in this moment, a final turn if there ever was one. No one would deny that they had been well and truly cornered. Pearl, meanwhile, had used up all her offensive spells. She had no further cards that would deal damage to Dax or Kelritch.

"I...end...my turn," she announced, and so her turn was over. Last Stand would inflict its penalty of twenty life, and Pearl would be out. She and Fay would lose. "I'm sorry, Fay," Pearl said, but the smile flickered across her face. She looked tired. She'd given everything she had. "I thought I could win without making you back me up. I guess I'm not quite experienced enough yet..."

"What're you talking about?" Fay asked, bestowing the golden-haired girl with a gigantic grin. "*We won*, Pearl! You're the best partner I could have asked for."

"What?!" Dax exclaimed.

Kelritch echoed, "Wha—?!"

They weren't the only ones who were shocked. All of the tens of thousands of spectators in the stadium doubted their own ears.

"Y-you can't be serious!" Kelritch shouted. "Pearl! You used all your offensive magic cards, I know you did! You even declared your turn over!" She was glaring daggers at Pearl.

"My last card," said Pearl, her fingers brushing the final card in her hand. "I finally met the activation requirements. I've been saving it all this time..." She looked up at the sky like she was remembering something that had happened long ago. "This is a card that calls to other cards."

The others gasped.

"I cast the High-Speed spell Encore. It allows me to add one card that's been discarded to the hangar to my hand!"

Encore was a spell Pearl had been holding since they'd been randomly dealt the five cards of their opening hands. A trump card.

"*I do have this High-Speed Magic one. That's pretty special.*"

"*Hm? 'May be activated only when you have five or less life remaining and when this is the only card in your hand.' Geez, that is tough!*"

Yet Pearl's life total at that moment was five—and this was the last card in her hand. A moment that had been foreshadowed from the first seconds of the game was finally coming to pass: she'd satisfied the stringent conditions to use the High-Speed spell Encore.

"The card I pick from the hangar is the Healer's Secret Spell, Heartache!"

The hangar was a shared space where used cards were sent. Pearl's chosen card floated up into her hand.

"But this is ludicrous!" Dax howled. "I don't even recognize that spell! How did it get into the hangar?!"

The arena buzzed—everyone had the same question as Dax.

Pearl had the powerful Encore card in her hand from the start of the game, but that last-ditch Healer's spell? The one big catch was that it had to be in the hangar before she could retrieve it with Encore.

"That's impossible!" Kelritch said, shock in her eyes. "Heartache? A Healer's Secret Spell? No such card was used in this game! It can't *be* in the hangar!"

Everyone agreed with her; no one could understand how Pearl had made the move she just had.

With one exception.

"Maybe I can shed a little light on this." From the first row of the spectator seating, a girl ran her fingers through her sparkling vermilion hair. Leshea gave everyone a girlish grin. "Don't tell me you all forgot. Fay sent an unused card to the hangar in Phase Two."

"Oh!" exclaimed the black-haired girl sitting beside Leshea. She jumped to her feet, completely fixated on the game. "I know what you mean! When Master Fay used Soul's Sacrifice!"

*"I discard one card from my hand. That card and Soul's Sacrifice both go in the hangar..."*

\*     \*     \*

It was Fay who had been holding Heartache. Another powerful card, likewise, dealt to him in the opening draw. But it was a dead card as far as the Traveler Fay was concerned. If it was going to be any use to them at all, he absolutely had to get it to Pearl somehow.

"Don't tell me...," Kelritch said, looking at him wide-eyed. "Fay! *This* is what your question on the first turn was about?"

"Yeah. What else?"

*"If one of us reaches zero life, we both lose. So what about our cards? Can we trade the magic cards in our hand?"*

It had all been a bluff. His question had planted a thought in the minds of everyone in the stadium: that he had no way to trade cards. If he'd had some card that would have enabled him to do so, he would never have asked.

But he *had* been holding such a card. He'd been able to give Pearl his card via the hangar.

"Your question had us believing in an illusion from the first turn!" Kelritch said.

"Oh, I wouldn't go that far. I just needed you guys to let your guard down a little."

Two players of Dax and Kelritch's caliber would of course be on the lookout for any attempt to pass cards via the hangar, but somewhere deep down inside, they had dismissed the possibility, wrongly convinced that the other team had no way of pulling off such a swap.

All because of one innocent question from Fay.

"Point of interest, but the reason I used Swords of the Heavenly Host just before that wasn't really about the damage. It was just to get you looking somewhere else before I dropped my cards into the hangar."

"I...I can't believe this!" Kelritch leaned forward. "With an eye on Phase Three, you discarded a card in Phase Two. And with an eye toward Phase Two, you asked a question in Phase One purely as a bluff!"

"You're giving me too much credit if you think I had it all figured out. I was just pushing our strategy forward as far as I could."

"What?"

"I said right when we chose our classes, didn't I? That Pearl and I had to make our stand and stick to our plan?"

The other two were left speechless.

"She and I were after damage all along."

Fay and Pearl. Dax and Kelritch. Their plans had been the same from the start. But where Dax and Kelritch had chosen the obvious route of playing Wizards, Fay and Pearl had committed to hiding their strategy from the moment they picked their classes.

"B-but why?! Why would you take such a roundabout, furtive approach?!" Kelritch choked out. "If damage was what you were after, why not just choose Wizards?"

"Well, we'd never have won then," Fay said.

"Come again...?"

"Our hands had a definite bias toward healing spells. Which implied that *your* hands might be loaded with offensive magic. If we just got into an arms race with the two of you, you would have torn us apart. We wouldn't have had enough attacking cards to keep up. A bit of a mind game was our only option."

Yes, the Wizard class would have been the obvious solution if they just wanted to do damage, but if they'd gone that route, then the clear advantage would have lied with Dax and Kelritch, who were pursuing the same strategy. So instead, Fay and Pearl had gambled everything, their very survival, on this single potent card.

**Healer's Secret Spell: Heartache.**
**Damage taken by a player is redirected. This damage**
**cannot be reduced.**

"*This* finally settles it!" Pearl said. She'd managed to cling to a total of three life—enough to use one last card. It would bring her to one life, to the very edge of destruction. Truly, this was her last resort.

*Secret Spell Heartache.* It would allow her to deflect the twenty damage done by Last Stand. Directly onto the young man in the black coat.

"I see. Very well, I forfeit. It seems I was still taking you too lightly. Stupendous work, Pearl Diamond."

The arena filled with light. The audience closed their eyes against the brightness, and when the light faded, they opened them and heard:

"Game Over. Dax's remaining life: zero. Fay and Pearl are the winners."

"W-we did it! Fay, we did it!" Pearl jumped up in the air. "We won! We beat the best team in Mal-ra! We... Huh? Fay? You don't look very... Uhh..."

Pearl blinked. It was only then that she looked around the stadium and realized. Their victory was greeted only by a smattering of applause. The cheering had all but stopped.

"Oh..." Pearl swallowed hard.

She was on the away team at Mal-ra's own stadium. Deep down, most of the spectators had probably been hoping that Dax would win on behalf of their city. They were less than wholeheartedly thrilled by Fay and Pearl's victory.

She soon had to think again, though.

"Heh... Ha-ha-ha! Ha-ha-ha-ha-ha-ha-ha-ha!"

The stadium rang with the laughter of the city's foremost apostle. His laughter was heartfelt, carefree. So boisterous that you would never have believed he'd just lost a game.

"I see now!" Dax crossed his arms and gave an exaggerated nod. But what did he see? Fay, the spectators, and even his partner Kelritch looked at him in puzzlement. "I understand!" he said and pointed at Fay. "Fay! I was right—you and I are destined to be rivals all our lives!"

There was a long pause, and then Fay said, "Pardon?"

"Our battle this day is indeed the beginning of destiny. The first act of our legend, which shall be forged over the course of many tens of thousands, even many millions of games!"

"Wait, how many?! Er... Never mind. I had fun, too."

"I knew my vision was unclouded." Dax nodded to himself. The foremost apostle of the Sacred Spring City of Mal-ra was extraordinarily pleased. "Therefore, spectators, I call on you to witness! I've vowed to be stronger tomorrow than I am today. My legend begins here!"

There was an instant of silence, and then tens of thousands of voices broke into a cheer of "Dax! Dax! Dax!" that shook the stadium.

"Umm... They lost, but it seems like they're the ones everyone is cheering for," Pearl said.

"It's all good. We got to have a fun game," Fay said. It was time to go. He glanced at Pearl and started walking toward the green room.

"Fay!" Dax shouted from behind him. "We shall meet again. Next time in the gods' games!"

"Come again?"

"You'll see soon enough. Let's be off, Kelritch," he said. With those portentous words, Dax Gear Scimitar turned and left the stadium, his coat billowing behind him as he went.

Vs. Dax and Kelritch—WIN
Game: Mind Arena
Time Elapsed: 1 hour, 5 seconds

Win Condition 1: Reach the goal line before the opposing team.
Win Condition 2: Reduce the opposing team's life to 0.

Dropped Item: Acknowledgment of lifelong rivalry from the apostle Dax
(Dropped on Difficulty: "...Dax looked like he was having fun for the first time in a long while." —Kelritch)

# Player.4
## Too Devout to Drop Out

# 1

On the day after the pride match—their third day in the Sacred Spring City of Mal-ra, Fay and his companions went sightseeing.

"Fay, look over here!" said Leshea, her eyes shining as she took in the main thoroughfare. They were in a shopping area, surrounded by game stores stocked with everything from classic board games to the latest game machines. "Ah! I'm in heaven... Ruin's game shops are great, but a new city means a new selection of merchandise. There are all these games I don't even recognize!"

"Ah! You've got fine taste for such a young lady," said an elderly proprietor who emerged from one of the stores, walking with a cane. The other shoppers all looked a little shocked by Leshea's presence; the old proprietor seemed to be the only one there who didn't realize she was a former god. "That game, the one you're holding—that's a legendary board game that I won at an auction. It was a limited edition; they only sold five hundred pieces worldwide."

"I'll take it!"

"I like your spirit. But I'm not quite sure you can afford it with your pocket change."

"Don't worry, I've got plenty in here." Leshea pulled out an adorable cat purse, then produced a sleek, black card—a platinum credit card issued by the Arcane Court, said to have no credit limit. A true one-off item, issued only to former gods. "You can put it on this card! Even if Miranda did tell me not to abuse it!"

"Hoh… Say, young lady, you might be interested to know that I got a shipment of game consoles in just yesterday. The hottest new thing—the Cwitch. But only three of 'em…"

"I'll take one!"

"And here's a beloved card game that won the Game Award ten years ago…"

"Gimme!" Leshea pressed the credit card into the man's hand. "Just ship everything in this store to the Sacrament City of Ruin!"

"Hey, Leshea, uh, you ready?" Fay asked.

"I am satisfied!" Leshea said, turning to him with her eyes shining.

From behind them they heard "Fay! Leshea! Sorry to keep you waiting!" as Pearl crossed the intersection. In her left hand she held a bag full of grilled potatoes, while in her right was a kebab sandwich. Fay wondered about them. "I'm treating myself a bit," Pearl explained, grinning broadly. "Something to say *Congratulations and thank you, Pearl, for overcoming that scorchingly intense battle yesterday!*"

"You do remember we had a celebratory dinner yesterday, right? And we just ate breakfast a few—"

"Welp, let's be on our way! Chief Secretary Baleggar gave me a great tip. He said the city's favorite takoyaki place is at the shopping mall next door!"

Pearl bounded off. Fay and Leshea made to follow her, but no sooner had they reached the intersection than they heard voices behind them.

"U-um, Honored Dragon God!"

"Lady Leoleshea!"

"Who, me?" Leshea said, turning. Several men wearing the outfits of Mal-ra apostles came running up. For some reason, all of them had their cameras out and were carrying autograph paper.

"Please take a picture with me!"

"A-and then me! Could we get a selfie together?"

"Maybe I could get your autograph? Enough for me and my team—that's seventeen copies!"

In the space of an instant, they were surrounded. Leshea looked bewildered, like a cornered animal. She didn't seem to grasp that the eager men were fans of hers. Fay and Pearl looked at the guys mobbing Leshea, then at each other. "Hey... Come to think of it, has this ever happened to Leshea before? You'd think she'd have fans at every turn, being a former god and all."

"Remember, Fay, in our city people are pretty afraid of her."

"Ahh... Yeah, guess you're right."

In Mal-ra, however, the people had no fear of Leshea. They didn't know about the "Day of the Blood-Soaked God," when she'd sent a whole group of apostles to the hospital for disparaging the gods' games. They'd never seen how dangerous she could be.

"Leshea's an awfully pretty face, after all," Pearl said.

"Maybe, but she sure doesn't seem to know what to do right now."

She wasn't used to being surrounded by male admirers. At that moment, she was squeezed between a couple of guys taking a photo, and the very fact that she didn't seem quite sure what she was doing gave her an adorable awkwardness.

"U-um! You're Fay, aren't you?" said a new voice.

"Huh?" Fay turned to find three girls just behind him. Judging by their outfits, they were ordinary citizens.

"W-we—! We were watching the game yesterday…!"

"You just looked so cool, the way you played! Please give us your autograph!"

"And pictures! Let's take pictures! And d-do you think we could shake your hand if we paid you?"

"Paid me?! Look, you don't have to…"

Even as Fay spoke, two more girls clutching autograph pads were working their way through the intersection.

"You've got to be kidding me! I don't even get this kind of treatment in Ruin!" Fay said.

"I-is this what it means to be a guest of the WGT?!" Pearl said, swallowing hard. They were famous visitors from another city. From Mal-ra's perspective, it was like a world-famous singer or some other star had come on tour. Big news. "Wait! Does that mean *I'll* be popular, too?!" Pearl's eyes widened. "I *was* the real star of yesterday's battle! Which means news of my exploits must be known far and wide! Pretty soon… Pretty soon people will wait in line for three hours for my signature, just like I was a popular theme park attraction! Come now, O fans of mine!"

The intersection was silent.

Pearl stood with her arms wide, prepared to welcome her throngs of admirers, but nobody went to her. In fact, she was getting some *what's-that-girl-doing?* looks.

"Uh…?"

"Maybe people didn't like the whole Pearl Fire thing."

"But it's such an awesome name! Urgh… If you need me, I'll be over there buying a crêpe or something…to make myself feel better…"

Pearl slunk away. She was replaced by Leshea, who appeared

to have successfully escaped from an excessive number of photo and autograph requests in the street.

"This is freaking me out!" she said.

"Yeah, you definitely looked pretty overwhelmed. I haven't done autographs for a long time myself. A few people asked me six months ago, but that's all."

"Oh! Your autograph!" Leshea said.

"Hm?" Fay hadn't thought his comment was that interesting, but Leshea's eyes were glowing with curiosity.

"I think *I* might just want your autograph, Fay!"

"Why?"

"It's human culture, right? Things that are autographed are saved and treasured. I can't believe that I, your very own teammate, haven't gotten a signature from you!" Well, this was unexpected. Leshea shoved the pen she'd been using to sign autographs herself until just a moment ago into Fay's chest. "Pretty please!"

"Sure. I mean, I don't mind, but...are you sure you want my autograph? Like, rationally?"

"Yours, yes. As proof of our friendship."

"You happen to have an autograph pad on you?"

"Nope."

"Figured. Maybe we can swing by a stationery store on the way home or something..."

*Tug.* Fay was about to walk away when Leshea grabbed his sleeve. "I want it now," she said.

"Yeah, but I mean, you don't..."

"I don't need it on any special paper. I wouldn't mind if it was right on my skin, where it would never leave me... Hey, that's it!" Leshea spun around and pointed to the green ribbon tying up her hair. "You can sign my ribbon!"

"When you want something, you really want it, huh? Not much space to write here. Wonder if I can even make it fit..."

"This feels much more, you know, unique to me, right?"

Slowly, hesitantly, Fay signed the ribbon. People in the street were looking at them. Honestly, he was a little embarrassed. But he said, "There, done."

"Yippee!" Leshea bounced into the air, her vermilion hair bouncing with her. Her fingers brushed the ribbon and she looked joyful. "I'll treasure this forever."

The former god's smile was so innocent, so childlike. She sounded so genuinely thrilled that Fay found himself blushing as she turned that radiant smile on him.

"What's wrong, Fay?" she asked.

"It's nothing, it's nothing," he said. Who knew that a real, live (albeit former) deity could get so excited about something so simple? That's what he was thinking. He was just trying to decide whether to say it out loud when—

"C'mon, what's keeping you two?" Pearl appeared behind him, gripping a freshly made (and freshly purchased) crêpe with both hands.

"Yikes!" Fay said.

"You were standing weirdly close together," Pearl observed.

"Aw, Leshea just wanted me to sign her—"

"Hey, let's not slack on the sightseeing!" Leshea exclaimed. She seemed eager to act like nothing was going on.

They were walking around the bustling city when Fay noticed that the middle of the street was packed. "Huh? What's going on over there?" he asked. It looked like there were hundreds of people gathered—most of them women.

He didn't have to listen hard to hear the cries of "Dax! I'm over here, my sweet Dax!" These girls were obviously smitten.

"Dax?!" Fay exclaimed. It was the young man in his black uniform, completely surrounded by female fans. The apostle walked down the street with his coat flapping dramatically. He was so handsome he could have been a model.

"Dax! Remember me? I was cheering for you from the second row in the stadium!"

"Daaax! You were *so awesome* in that battle yesterday!"

"Ohmygosh! He *looked* at me!"

Every time Dax took a step, somebody shouted or cried out. He hardly seemed to notice; simply strode ahead. He was going to an obviously extravagant restaurant.

"It can't be!" Pearl cried. "Is this... It must be twelve fifteen in the afternoon! Am I right, Fay?!"

"What's all this about?" Fay asked.

"I happened to learn something when I was looking at a 'lunch map' of the city. I'm sure he's going to film *Dax's Lunch*!"

"And, uh...what's that, Pearl?"

"It's a broadcast of him eating lunch."

"That's it?!"

"You don't understand! Tens of thousands of fans log on to watch him eat in real time! Rumor has it that broadcast alone brings in twice as much money as an apostle's salary!"

"That's completely insane!"

"It shows you how popular he is." The comment came not from Fay or either of his companions, but from the tan girl who'd appeared directly beside them. "You must have guessed from all the cheering yesterday. You must've realized how beloved Dax is."

"Yikes! I mean, uh, Kelritch..."

"Fine work in our game," she said with a polite bow. Her impassive expression never shifted, however. Then she continued, "He's whip-smart, an excellent athlete, tall and handsome, outgoing, and always considerate toward his teammates. One of the best game players around. How could he not be popular?"

"Well, look who's got a honey tongue."

"I'm only telling you what other women say about him. To me, Dax is a business partner, no more and no less. And now I bid you good day."

With that, Kelritch walked away. She seemed to be keeping a discreet eye on Dax as the ladies mobbed him. To Fay and his friends, it seemed perfectly obvious that she was tailing him because she was bothered by the situation. But anyway, it wasn't their job to stick their noses in.

"Are *all* the apostles in this city so...quirky?" Pearl asked, trading a look with Leshea.

Fay turned abruptly. "I don't know. What do *you* think, Nel?"

A dark-haired girl observing them from the shadows of a building jumped, nearly choking. She soon got herself under control, though, and with a look of resolve she said, "Master Fay! Y-your play in yesterday's match was extraordinary. It only renewed my conviction that I want to help you in any way I can!" She pressed a hand to her chest emphatically. "I beg you. I was defeated by the gods and can no longer play in the games myself, but I want to be your analyst. I want to help your team!"

Fay was somewhat lost for words.

"Master Fay!"

"Thanks, but no thanks," he said.

"Wha—?!" Nel looked stricken, but Fay insisted:

"I can't accept *that* proposal."

"W-well, then!" Nel said, clenching her fist, evidently inspired afresh. "In th-that case, how about as a housekeeper?! I'll do your cooking, your cleaning, your laundry—everything!"

"Yeah, no." This time it was Leshea who shot Nel down, without so much as a second's thought.

Nel's eyes grew distant. She looked at the ground, biting her lip. Then she said, ".........I see......" She turned away, still gazing at her feet. "I've made myself too pathetic to bear. I'm sorry for wasting your time." She began to trudge back toward the main street, swaying, as if her legs might give out at any moment.

*Ah*, Fay thought. Nel still wasn't getting it. She didn't understand *what* he and Leshea were refusing. She wasn't pathetic. She was *too pure-hearted.*

"Nel," Fay said. "Would you really be satisfied with that?"

She caught her breath.

"An analyst? A housekeeper? Cleaning and cooking and laundry and whatever?" Fay sighed, scratching the back of his head awkwardly. Nel whipped around toward him. "Is that it? Is that what you *really* want to do?"

"I—I don't know what you mean, Master Fay!"

"Anyway, it's fine. I know it can't be easy to say it yourself." He looked at Leshea and then Pearl. Then he pointed in the direction of the Arcane Court building. "We're supposed to show up tomorrow at one in the afternoon. In the Dive Center on the first basement level."

"What? Master Fay, wait! What are you talking about?!" Nel didn't even try to hide her bewilderment.

"Us, we've got more sightseeing to do. Make sure you're there tomorrow, okay?" Fay said, and then stepped into the crosswalk.

# 2

WGT, day four.

They were in the basement of the Arcane Court Mal-ra branch office.

"So the day has come," Chief Secretary Baleggar said as he emerged from the emergency staircase. "Lady Leoleshea. My good sir, Fay. Pearl. It's time for another game. And this one's the real thing."

"Why am I the only one who doesn't get a title?!" Pearl exclaimed.

"A battle of wits with the gods!" Baleggar proclaimed, pointing at the center of the room. There stood a Divine Statue. Ruin's statues were all in the form of huge dragons, but Mal-ra's was carved in the likeness of the spirit Undine. The spirit held a water jug from which sparkling water flowed, almost blinding in its brilliance.

This was a gate to the gods' world. Pass through the light, and you would find yourself in Elements, the superior spiritual realm.

"The whole world will be watching the stream. I understand that even your chief secretary is tuning in from Ruin," Baleggar said. Then the big man in sunglasses cast a look at Fay. "Fay... You currently run a three-person team. In order to bring you up to headquarters' recommended minimum of ten people, we've chosen twelve apostles from our own branch office. All passionate young go-getters."

"So, fifteen people including us?"

"That's right. As you obviously know, the gods' games are usually contested by teams of at least twenty, but when a team's never worked together before, a larger number can make things worse instead of better. We tried to keep it small."

"Thank you, sir."

"Mm-hmm. They've already dove in."

So there were twelve people already waiting for them in Elements. Once Fay and his companions entered the gate, chances were the game would begin immediately.

A squeak came from a corner of the room. "U-um, Chief Secretary...?" Nel was there, dressed in civilian clothing and looking very awkward. Her fists were clenched. "I'm n-not sure why I'm here. I'm already retired, and I feel a little weird being back in the Dive Center..."

"I'm sure you'd like to observe the match. Fay told me."

"Master Fay..." Nel, still clearly uncomfortable, looked toward him. "I spent all last night thinking about it, but I still don't understand what you were getting at yesterday."

"The ones who cheer you on from right by your side—they're your teammates, right?" Fay said.

Nel gasped.

"I know you're unhappy that rooting for us is all you can do right now. But for the moment, I just want you to trust—and cheer."

"Wha—? Master Fay, what does that mean?! You're still not making any—"

"Okay, here we go!" called Leshea, her voice ringing around the Dive Center, clear and eager. "Let the game begin!"

"St-stop! Leshea, please don't push me!" said Pearl, who almost tumbled head over heels into the gate as Leshea shoved her from behind. The former god promptly followed.

"Master Fay!" Nel said, her voice still an octave higher than normal. "I—I still don't know what you want. What you're trying to say. But it doesn't matter. As long as I'm here, I promise I'll root for you with all my might!"

"Yeah. *Right back at you.*" Fay gave her a firm nod—and then jumped toward the Undine statue.

Elements: Ancient Battlefield of Trackless Sand

Vs. The God of the Sun Army, Mahtma II
Let the game begin.

**Nel**

Master Fay's game is finally underway...

**Chief Secretary Baleggar**

Yeah. And with it, the main event of this WGT. We picked our best apostles. Now all we can do is cheer them on.

**Nel**

Chief Secretary...I have a question.

**Chief Secretary Baleggar**

Yeah?

**Nel**

Why are you the only one who doesn't make an appearance on camera, sir?

**Chief Secretary Baleggar**

I did once. It made all the children watching the stream cry. I decided to stick with this icon after that.

**Nel**

You do look a little scary, sir.
(In fact, I think Pearl is a bit intimidated by you...)

**Chief Secretary Baleggar**

Well anyway, eyes up! It's starting!

# Player.5
## The Choice to Challenge the Gods

# 1

The gods on high invited people to play their games. Those whom they chose became apostles and could venture into the superior spiritual realm, Elements. But the apostles never knew what manner of place would be waiting for them; what kind of game they would be asked to play.

This time...

As Fay and the others came dropping in, they found themselves in a sandy desert that seemed to go on forever.

The ground was uniformly the color of...well, sand. It was dunes as far as the eye could see, under a completely clear blue sky. The scene was split; piercing azure above, and unending sandy hue below. So this was where Fay found himself today. It looked like the whole world was made of sand.

"Phew... At least we didn't start with a gigantic plummet like we did with Uroboros," Pearl said as she landed on the fine sand.

Soon, however, she looked up at the sky. "It's so hot! Why does the sunlight have to burn like that?!"

"Yep. This is a real desert all right," Fay said. The sun over their heads threatened to bake them. They seemed to be in a world of heat. The sand underfoot felt as hot as a frying pan, while the sun above beat down with murderous intensity.

"Huh! A desert playing field!" Leshea said, not sounding the least bit concerned. It was like the searing rays didn't even bother her. "I wonder what kind of game this is. Hey, Fay, maybe we should play a game of 'try to guess what kind of game this is' while we wait."

"Not a bad idea, but I think it would be better to introduce ourselves first." He looked around the desert, trying to find the twelve apostles who had gotten here ahead of him. "Leshea, can you, like, sense human presences or whatever?"

"I don't have to sense anything. You can hear footsteps right over that hill," she said, pointing.

At that moment, almost as if on cue, someone shouted, "I've been waiting for you, Fay!" From the far side of the dune appeared a young man in a black coat. "Today, I want you to show me just how good a teammate you can be!"

"A pleasure to be working with you," said Kelritch, trotting after Dax across the sand. Ten more people, a mix of men and women, came into view behind them.

"Hello, Honored Dragon God Leoleshea. And Fay and Pearl." A young woman with wavy brown hair bowed politely. She wore glasses and had sharp, intelligent eyes. Her height made her look very mature. "It's my pleasure to be joining you today as one of Mal-ra's chosen apostles. Today we have Dax and Kelritch from team Tempest Cruiser. I'm Camilla, and I run the team the other ten of us are from..."

"Team Archangel! Their motto is 'The great angels,'" Dax said.

"Dax! How could you steal the best part?!"

"They're only here to make up the numbers," Dax remarked.

"Can you *get* any ruder?!" Camilla cried.

"Fay!" Dax bellowed, Camilla's protestations no more than the gusting of the wind to him. "Even the games of the gods themselves are merely a stage for you and me to settle things between us! At least, I wish that were so..." His voice got quieter. "This is *your* turn on the WGT. It's not for me and Kelritch to steal the limelight."

"Huh? Who are you, and what have you done with Dax?" said Camilla. She might have been his colleague, but she seemed suitably astonished by his admission. "I've never known you to see yourself as anything but the star of every game you enter."

Dax sighed softly. "I bet, and I lost. The condition was that I do any one thing I was asked."

"Come again?"

"Nothing." He looked back at Fay. "I have high hopes for your performance today, Fay."

"Huh? Oh, yeah. I'll just try to do what I always do."

"Excellent, then!" Dax's coat flared as he pointed up toward the heavens and called out, "The stage is set! Come forth, O god!"

"I thought you *weren't* going to make yourself the center of attention?!" Fay jibed.

At that moment, though, there was a *boom* from behind him and the ground began to quake so violently that Fay and the others thought the earth might simply tear itself apart. And then, as they watched, something began to emerge in front of them.

"A pyramid?" Fay said. From out of the sand came a huge, golden, four-sided pyramid. As it rose up, something came down from overhead...

*     *     *

*"Many greetings! Welcome to my god's Elements!"*

A tiny, orange, winged humanoid descended toward them. *"I am the meep who resides in the territory of Mahtma II, the ruling deity here. A pleasure to meet all of you!"*

Meeps, or terminal spirits, were the intermediaries who taught apostles the rules of the games. Fay noticed that the instant she saw this one, Camilla of Team Archangel looked distinctly relieved.

*The gods with the hardest games sometimes deliberately choose not to provide a meep—like Uroboros.*

But this god had. An experienced apostle would immediately guess that the deity whose game they were in had a modicum of compassion for their human opponents.

Or so Fay might have thought. But then the meep said, *"Fifteen? That's all of you? Hmm..."* It looked down at them and considered. *"That's a couple digits short of what my master had in mind. But, oh well. It's time to start, so no additional participants will be allowed to join."*

"Wait, what did you just—" Fay said, but the meep cut him off.

*"All right, let's talk rules!"* The meep spread its arms, and a blizzard of blossoms came blowing across the desert. *"Excellent and very well! Firstly, as a sign of friendship, a flower for each of you."*

The flowers that came blowing through were as white as snow. The meep began passing out branches each with a large bud just about to bloom. First it handed one to Fay, then to the other fourteen people.

*Naturally, the branches figure into the game somehow. I can't help noticing that they're not flowers—they're buds that are about to be flowers,* Fay thought.

*"Take good care of your branch,"* the meep said. *"If you lose*

*it, you're out."* Its voice resounded around the desert. *"Those are just buds you've got there, but when they bloom, the flowers can be one of three colors."*

**Sun Flower (gold)—A flower offered on the altar of the sun. One for each team.**
**Poison Flower (black)—One for each team.**
**Sand Flower (white) —All others. (In other words, Fay and his companions will have 13 of them.)**

*"Perhaps you'd like to know what this game is called. Well, it's the Sunsteal Scramble! Your goal is to offer the Sun Flower on the altar on the uppermost level of the pyramid!"* The meep pointed toward the horizon, where the recently emerged pyramid shimmered like a mirage, far in the distance.

"So that's where we're headed," Fay said. All right. How far was it? The heat haze made it hard to judge, but even just eyeballing it, Fay figured it must be at least several kilometers. *And we're in a desert. Nothing harder to run on than sand. Even if it was just two kilometers away, it would take Pearl and me a good ten minutes or more to get there.*

For Leshea, however, or for an apostle with a Superhuman ability, it might be different. They might reach the pyramid in five minutes or less.

The meep seemed to know exactly what the humans were thinking. It said, *"As you may guess, my master's team is on defense."* It pointed at the pyramid again. *"Everyone on the defending team will be trying to steal your flowers away from you. If your flower gets stolen, you'll have to drop out—but don't lose hope. You can take their flowers as well."*

"And who or what exactly does your master's team consist of?" Fay asked.

*"Well, let me introduce you. Come out, O beasts formed by the hand of my master!"*

The dunes trembled. The sand began to rise up, then come together as if it had a will of its own, forming golems in the shapes of wild animals.

"Mrrah!"

"Mrrroww!" the beasts said.

"Hey... Those are cats!" Fay said.

"Oh my gooooosh! They're sooo cute!" Pearl gushed.

They were, in short, cat golems. They were pudgy and roly-poly, like cats who had learned to walk upright on their stubby legs, waving their little forepaws in the air. Their faces were like exaggerated adorable kittens. The golems lacked anything you might call an intimidation factor.

There were three of them, and as they came bounding across the sand, kicking up a dust cloud behind them, Fay and the others began to frown.

"They're...huge!" he exclaimed. They had to be more than two meters tall, larger than any of the humans. Taking width and length into account, they had to weigh well over a hundred kilograms each.

"O-oh... They're not so cute when you see them up close...," Pearl said, looking at the sand golems. "So these cat, uh, golems... they're here to keep us from getting to the pyramid?"

*"Precisely. They'll attack you and try to steal your flowers. As I mentioned, however, my master's team also possesses Sun Flowers. One possible approach would involve trying to take the beasts' blossoms away."*

Each of the sand creatures wore a collar around its neck, on which could be seen a flower bud. The humans could take the beasts out of the game by getting it from them.

"Wait a second. Hold on," Pearl said, cocking her head. "Is this what you would call Capture the Flag? It is, isn't it, Fay?"

"Might be," he said. Known by terms like "area-control games" or "flag games," it was a concept that could be found in many games: the contest to control territory, or one or more objects.

*So if a player's flower is stolen, they have to leave the playing field. And if your team's Sun Flower gets snatched, the whole team loses.* There was a psychological element to this battle—to these three kinds of flowers. The Sun Flower, and then the other two...

"Oh, hey!" Leshea said, beckoning to the meep where it floated in midair. "Tell us about the other two flowers. How about the Sand Flower first?"

*"You could think of it as a kind of camouflage. Stealing it or having it stolen from you doesn't grant victory or inflict a loss."*

"What about the Poison Flower, then?"

*"If either team is unfortunate enough to steal that, they incur divine punishment—in the form of a debuff—a negative status effect. The bearer of their Sun Flower is revealed, and additionally the entire team is stunned for five seconds."*

"In other words, it's basically an invitation to try to get the other team to take your Poison Flower," Leshea said, folding her arms and thinking. "Should we understand 'stunned' to mean you can't move?"

*"That's right. You can't move, attack, or defend. This applies to either team if they grab the wrong flower."*

That was why they were buds. You wouldn't know which flower you'd taken—Sun, Poison, or Sand—until after you'd taken it.

"Five seconds," Pearl mused, looking worried. "I run the fifty-meter dash in nine seconds, so in half that time, I guess I could get about twenty meters away. A nice, safe distance...if we can get them to take our Poison Flower."

"Say, Pearl," Fay said.

"Yes?"

"Have you ever played any RTS games? You know, real-time strategy? Or any shooters?"

"Oh, uh, n-no. I don't really have the reflexes for them..."

"Well, in an RTS, a five-second stun would be a death sentence."

"Whaaat?!"

"Just imagine if they let Leshea go hog wild for five whole seconds. We'd have the win in the bag, right?"

"Oh... I guess you're right..."

In five seconds, Leshea could probably steal every flower from every one of the opposing team's members. Five seconds in the gods' games was critical.

*And we're in the same kind of danger. If we make the mistake of taking their Poison Flower, it's pretty much over.*

They had to protect the Sun Flower with their lives, and try to devise a way to get the other team to take their Poison Flower. It would be acting ability versus deductive reasoning; it was a test of whether each team could work out who was holding what.

"Where is this master of yours, anyway?" Fay asked.

*"The god who is my master will appear when your strategy meeting is over."* In other words, Mahtma II wasn't going to cheat by eavesdropping on their plans. That was sporting, in a godly way. Even the beasts were keeping a respectful distance.

"Gotcha. All right, then... By the way, you passed these flowers out randomly, right? You don't mind if we tell each other who has what?"

*"Go right ahead. You can nudge open the buds."*

Fay gently lifted a petal of his flower. The one he'd received was white.

*It's one of the Sand Flowers. So who's got the Sun and Poison Flowers?*

"I—I have the Sun Flower!" Pearl said. Golden petals glittered in her hand.

"And I have the Poison Flower," said Kelritch. It was a deep black, like some kind of poisonous mushroom. The other thirteen apostles all had Sand Flowers.

*"You're all aware of who has which flower now, yes? Time to swap, then! Think carefully about who you want carrying what."*

All right. They needed to get their thoughts together. The Sunsteal Scramble had three win/lose conditions.

> **Win Condition 1: Run to the pyramid and place the Sun Flower on the highest level.**
> **Win Condition 2: Steal the god team's Sun Flower.**
> **Lose Condition 1: The human team's Sun Flower is stolen.**

It was several thousand meters to the pyramid that loomed on the horizon. Getting there would mean a race across the desert, with the god and their beasts trying to stop the apostles every step of the way.

"About these beasts...," Fay started.

"They're cat golems, Fay," Pearl advised him.

"Uh, all right. About these cat golems. They look like they'd move pretty quick."

They might be cute enough to steal Pearl's heart, but they were more than two meters tall. Even these oversized plush toys could gain enough speed to kick up a dust cloud.

*We'll have to factor in how we get away from those things, too. In a straight foot race, a Magical Arise might be a liability.* If they were just going to sprint across the sand away from the creatures, it would be all about physical capacity. Apostles with Arises granting physical enhancements would have a better chance. Which raised the question, who was the right person to hold their Sun Flower?

"Actually, I guess it should be obvious," Fay said. As he looked around at the other fourteen of them, he couldn't suppress a smile—because they were all looking at the same person. Leshea.

A Superhuman apostle would be a good choice, of course, but even they couldn't hold a candle to a former god. Even if the beasts somehow surrounded her, they wouldn't find it so easy to pry her flower from her.

"Hey, Fay," Leshea said. She pointed at Kelritch's Poison Flower. "Having me hold the Sun Flower is great and all, but don't you think giving me this one would be even *more* interesting?"

The god's team would almost certainly guess that Leshea would be holding the Sun Flower—which meant that turning that expectation on its head by giving her the Poison Flower instead could be a potent ploy.

"Okay, so if we give Leshea the Poison Flower, who gets the Sun Flower? I think giving it to a Superhuman would be ideal for this game. Anyone here fit the bill?"

Several hands went up. Dax's wasn't one of them, suggesting he had a Magical Arise.

The girl standing beside Dax, though—she raised her hand.

"Huh?" Fay said.

"Don't look at me like that. Are you that shocked that I have a Superhuman Arise?" Kelritch said.

Kelritch—of all people! Superhuman Arises usually involved extraordinary physical abilities. Fay had had the taciturn young woman pegged as a mage from the first time they'd met. But he'd been wrong.

"Yeah... Pretty shocked, yeah."

"If you're curious, my Arise is the ability to instantaneously strengthen my body. I'm also trained in self-defense. If I may be so bold, I might not be such a bad choice to take the Sun Flower myself."

"Got it. I'll keep that in mind."

Leshea with the Poison Flower. Kelritch with the Sun Flower. *I think that seems like the most viable strategy. The real Achilles' heel is that makes it the easiest for the opposing team to decode, too.* It would be obvious precisely because it was the best strategy. And this was the gods' games. It wasn't going to be easy—Fay didn't expect to have much hope of victory if the other side figured out their plan.

"Hey, can we trade flowers during the game?" Fay asked.

"*It's allowed, but you have to be careful,*" the meep replied. "*Once the game starts, if there's even an instant when you're not carrying a flower, you're considered to have lost your flower and you're out on the spot.*"

"So if we tried to toss our buds to each other..."

"*That would definitely cause you to be flower-free, and that'd be it. I'd watch out if I were you.*"

Fay spent a moment in quiet thought. At length he said, "Interesting. So transfer is allowed."

"*How do you mean, transfer?*"

"Like, say a player in a tight spot tosses their flower to someone else."

"*Ah, yes. That would be permitted. The player without a flower would immediately be removed from the game, of course.*"

But unilateral transfers were acceptable. In principle, it would be within the rules to give all fifteen of their flowers to Leshea.

*The risk would be too high, though. You couldn't make it more obvious who had the Sun Flower.*

They would consider "transferring" flowers a last resort. This game was designed to encourage all fifteen of them to work together flawlessly, as a team.

*That's one major difference from the games with Uroboros or Titan: you can't get away with solo play. We all have to protect the Sun Flower, at any cost.*

Dax and Kelritch were here, along with ten apostles from Camilla's Archangel team. It was the first time Fay had met most of them, but they were going to need to be in perfect sync to pull this off.

Dax folded his arms and closed his eyes. "You make the call, Fay," he said. He sounded like he knew this was deadly serious. "This is your game with the gods. You pick who takes the Sun Flower and who takes the Poison Flower."

"Dax! There *is* something wrong with you today, I know it!" Camilla said, wheeling toward him. She looked incredulous. "Normally you'd be all, 'None but I could possibly take the Sun Flower!'"

"No, I wouldn't."

"Yes, you would! A-anyway, what's going on? I know! You've got your tail between your legs because he beat you in your game a couple days ago! That's why you're being so nice to him."

"Hah!" Dax burst out. "Would I do such a thing? Surely you jest, Camilla. I would never debase myself like that."

"W-well, what is it, then? What's with you today?"

"I already told you. I made a promise to do any one thing I was told."

Camilla only gave him a puzzled look. Dax continued, "Right

now, however, that is of no significance. At this moment, what interests me most is to see how my peerless, one and only rival will comport himself against a god."

Fay had apparently gone from the Dax's lifelong rival to his "one and only rival." Was that a promotion?

"Okay, whatever. If you're going to be calling the strategy, Fay, you might want to know what Arises we have." Camilla took out an IC card containing a list of Archangel's apostles. It included all ten of the people there, including Camilla, giving their win-loss record in the gods' games and details about their Arise abilities. Fay took a quick glance at it on an Arcane Court device.

"Thanks, I think I've got it," he said.

"Already?!"

"Yeah, but we still haven't made the most important decision."

Who would take the Sun Flower and who the Poison one? The obvious picks would be Leshea and Kelritch, respectively. For one thing, Kelritch would be more conversant with Archangel's abilities than Fay was. She'd said it "might not be such a bad choice" to give her the Poison Flower. Fay wasn't sure how much to read into that.

"All right, I've made up my mind," Fay said, nodding at the others. "For starters, I want all of you to give your flowers to me for a minute."

They passed him their flowers, and he shuffled them so that only he knew which was which. Then he handed them back out.

"Now I want you to look at your flowers just like we did before. *But don't let anyone see what you have.*"

There was some gasping and *Oh!*-ing as people looked at their flowers. Everyone seemed to have about the same reaction. Pearl swallowed heavily, while Leshea giggled to herself. Dax stood silently with his arms folded, while Kelritch could be heard to murmur, "So it's come to that." Camilla was frowning, too, as if she was starting to suspect what was going on.

"My strategy begins now," Fay said. "As for exactly what that strategy is..."

With everyone watching him, he turned toward the pyramid behind him, looming on the horizon. *This is the Sunsteal Scramble. Unlike with Titan or Uroboros, we know the rules from the outset.*

They had to get their flower to the pyramid. There would be unexpected twists, no doubt, but what the humans needed to do to win was clear enough.

Camilla spoke up. "All we really have to do is run toward that pyramid as fast as we can, right? As long as we get there, that's what counts. We all focus on protecting whoever has the Sun Flower. And if things really get tight, that person can always toss the flower to someone else."

"Yeah. That would be the obvious approach," Fay said.

"All right. So we need to know who has the Sun Flower."

"No. It's better you don't."

"What?"

"It's key to my strategy. I'm not telling anyone where the Sun Flower is."

*"What?!"*

Camilla was about to demand to know what was going on, but before she could get the words out, Fay continued, "If everyone knew who had the Sun Flower, they'd flock to protect them. The god's team would see where it was right away, right?"

If Fay's team knew where the Sun Flower was, the god would soon know, too. Conversely, if Fay kept the flower's location a secret even from his friends, then his opponents couldn't figure it out, either.

*Both approaches have their advantages and disadvantages—but I think the second method might have a better chance in this game.*

That was his hypothesis. Why? Because the god's team knew what they were doing. The game was *called* Sunsteal Scramble. Which implied Mahtma had a lot more experience stealing Sun Flowers than Fay did protecting them. He needed a new strategy, one the god wouldn't have seen before.

"The only people who know where the Sun Flower is are me and the person who has it. In a word, I want *all* of you to run for that pyramid like you're holding the Sun Flower. We're going to trick this god."

*"All right!"* the meep said cheerily. *"Thank you for your patience. My master, the magnificent deity Mahtma II, has arrived!"*

A humanlike silhouette appeared on the dunes: a god wearing a mask made to look like a falcon and carrying a shining staff.

*"Are you ready for the game?"*

"Yikes! Wh-what's happening? It's like my ears, they..." Pearl pressed her hands against her ears, but this was not a voice that was carried through the air. It was a direct communication from the god that seemed to pound its way into the brains of Fay and his companions.

"Telepathy?" Fay said. That was something the gods could do to communicate directly with humans. Few of the gods went out of their way to use human language, and telepathy served as a good substitute.

"U-um!" Pearl said, looking up at the deity who stood upon the dunes. "There's something I really, really want to ask you, honored god. If you're Mahtma II, does that mean there's a Mahtma I?"

*"There is not."*

"Well, that doesn't make much sense!"

*"This entire world is but a game—my name included."*

The god raised its staff. At the end was a glass ball containing a flower bud just like the ones Fay and his teammates had been given. *So that's Mahtma's flower. I'd say there's a nine out of ten chance the god has the Sun Flower.*

Given that losing your Sun Flower meant immediate defeat, it seemed ridiculous that the god would take anything else. The way Mahtma raised that staff, the flower plainly visible, radiated confidence: *Go ahead and take it, if you can,* it seemed to say.

Perfect. If that was how Mahtma wanted to play, then Fay was happy to make this game all about exploiting that mechanic.

*"The game now begins. I urge you, humans, to play with all your wit and all your..."* Mahtma II trailed off, its telepathy ceasing. The falcon mask looked downward. *"Human. What is that you are doing? What action are you taking?"*

"Exactly what it looks like," Fay said.

"The game's started, right? So have we!" added Leshea. What they said next, stark in the great desert around them, was a shock not just to the god, but to all the tens of thousands of spectators watching the game.

"I've got the Sun Flower!" said Fay.

"I've got the Sun Flower!" said Leshea.

———————

In the Ruin branch office of the Arcane Court, in her office on the seventh floor, Chief Secretary Miranda clutched her head and cried out, "Arrrrrrrrgh!"

She pressed her hands to the monitor hanging on the wall, staring fixedly at the young man and woman on-screen.

"Wh-what do you think you're doing, Fay?! Lady Leshea?! What game are you playing?!"

If the god's team took their Sun Flower, the match would be over on the spot. That was the whole point of the strategy Fay had devised, to make sure nobody knew who had the Sun Flower. And *this* was the first thing they did?!

"Why would you *tell* them that?! What happened to the *plan*?!"

Miranda was chief secretary of an Arcane Court office. She understood what these two were angling at. She wasn't sure she could guess exactly what they were thinking, but she knew they had to be thinking *something*. Even so, though...

"To be so bold right in the middle of the real thing..." She sat down heavily on the sofa, pulled up her knees, and sighed ceilingward. "At least they'll catch that god by surprise. Because if I know one thing, it's that Fay and Lady Leshea didn't work this out ahead of time. They're improvising."

———————

At the same moment, in the Mal-ra branch office, some astonished viewers were looking at a screen in the Dive Center in the first basement, the one with the Undine statue.

"Master Fay!" Nel couldn't keep the name from bursting from her lips as she watched the young man in the desert. "What in the world are you planning?!"

What was going on? She of all people should have been able to parse the game she was seeing, but she just couldn't make sense of it.

"I mean, the announcement is one thing—but how can both of them do it?" There was only one Sun Flower, yet they had both said they had it. "One of them must be lying," Nel concluded.

> Possibility 1: Fay was lying, and Leshea had the Sun Flower.
> Possibility 2: Leshea was lying, and Fay had the Sun Flower.

"My guess is…either Master Fay or Lady Leshea has the Sun Flower, but the other one has the Poison Flower!"

Fay had turned the game into a giant gamble. The god's team could win by taking the humans' Sun Flower, meaning they had to get the bloom from either Fay or Leshea. And if they chose wrong, they would wind up with the Poison Flower.

"Nel," said Chief Secretary Baleggar. He sounded contemplative. "I think there's a ninety percent chance you're correct, but have you considered a third possibility?"

> Possibility 3: Fay and Leshea are both lying, and one of the remaining thirteen apostles had the Sun Flower.

"Yes, sir, of course that's conceivable, but…" She bit her lip, but not out of disappointment or frustration. It was because she couldn't stop the trembles of excitement passing through her. She couldn't wait to see just how far Fay and Leshea's plans would surpass their spectators' expectations! "But if one of the other thirteen apostles has the Sun Flower, then this is a much weaker gambit to induce the other team to take the Poison Flower."

Fay's and Leshea's announcements were an attempt to force the enemy into a choice: go after one of them or the other. If one of them had the Sun Flower and the other the Poison Flower, and if getting the opponent to take the Poison Flower meant almost certain victory, that gave them a fifty-fifty shot. Considering that the typical chance of a human victory in the gods' games hovered in the ten-percent range, it was a gamble more than worth taking.

But…was it really? Something nagged at Nel, a feeling that something was slightly out of place. Something that seemed like it could turn everything she was thinking inside out. Her whole body felt hot; her veins coursed with a premonition that they still had another surprise up their sleeve.

"Master Fay, I can't wait to see what it is!"

———————

At that moment, there was no one who fully understood what Fay was trying to do. Not among the global viewing audience, not among the members of Team Archangel, not even Pearl or Kelritch. In fact, there was something they were all overlooking. Something down in the corner of the giant monitor, somewhere beyond Fay and Leshea.

"Hmph. Very well. I'll play along with your little game, Fay."

They were overlooking the smile on the face of Mal-ra's foremost apostle, Dax. Had they noticed it, it would have looked very strange. But he, and he alone in all the world, had arrived at the conclusion before anyone else.

Possibility 1: Fay was lying, and Leshea had the Sun Flower.
Possibility 2: Leshea was lying, and Fay had the Sun Flower.
Possibility 3: Fay and Leshea are both lying, and one of the remaining 13 apostles had the Sun Flower.

The answer was actually…possibility four. This game, this challenge against a god, was going to revolve around a possibility that shouldn't have existed.

# 2

The desert was so hot, the very air itself seemed to be scorched. There under the gaze of the god Mahtma II, virtually everyone except Fay and Leshea stood with their mouths agape. Privately, Fay gave himself a mental pat on the back. *This is exactly what I wanted. If I can't even keep my friends off-balance, I'll never pull the wool over a god's eyes!*

If there was one thing he hadn't been counting on, it was that Leshea would say the exact same thing as him at the exact same time. Under normal circumstances, he would have handled the entire strategy himself. But oh well—this just made things more interesting.

*Leshea's declaration and mine might sound the same at first blush—but we're after completely different things.*

With that in mind, Fay looked up at the creator of this Elements, the falcon-masked god Mahtma II. The three beasts made of sand stood ready behind the deity. "What happened to starting the game? Or can we go ahead and get running for the pyramid?" he said.

*"Meep! Ring the bell."*

*"I'm on it! All right, everyone, it's the moment you've all been waiting for!"*

The meep darted down through the air with a small bell in its hand, which it waved with a forceful yet delicate motion.

*Ding!*

*"And we're off and running! Or at least, you are!"*

Then everything happened at once. Fay and the fourteen others went dashing for the pyramid, but at the same time the god raised the staff in its hand.

*"Come to me, my army. Summon Cats!"*

The desert heaved, the earth quaking so violently that Fay

could feel it even as far as he was from Mahtma. The sand by the god's feet started to rise, gathering and coalescing into another bipedal beast.

"Mrrow!"

"Oh! Another sweet cat golem!"

"Uh, why do you sound so happy about that, Pearl?"

"I mean, it's just so cute!" She looked back over her shoulder as they ran, where they could see huge quantities of sand gathering, forming more beasts.

"Mrrow!" "Mrrow!"

"Mrrow!" "Mrrow!" "Mrrow!" "Mrrow!" "Mrrow!" "Mrrow!" "Mrrow!" "Mrrow!" "Mrrow!" "Mrrow!" "Mrrow!"

"Okay, hold on..."

"Mrrow!" "Mrrow!" "Mrrow!" "Mrrow!" "Mrrow!" "Mrrow!" "Mrrow!" "Mrrow!" "Mrrow!" "Mrrow!" "Mrrow!" "Mrrow!" "Mrrow!" "Mrrow!" "Mrrow!" "Mrrow!" "Mrrow!" "Mrrow!" "Mrrow!" "Mrrow!" "Mrrow!"

"That is *way* too many cats!" Fay shouted—and they were still coming. The dunes were practically invisible, covered by cat golems.

"*A fine sight*," proclaimed Mahtma II, looking with pleasure upon the army it had summoned. Fay was reminded of what the meep had said before the beginning of the game. About their team being a couple digits short...

Mahtma said, "*Fifteen pawns against 1,667. A good, fair fight.*"

"How is that fair?!" Fay cried, his lament joining those of fourteen other apostles that echoed across the desert.

Vs. Mahtma II, the God of the Sun Army

Let the game begin!

# Player.6
## Where Has the Sun Gone?

# 1

According to the Arcane Court's shared database, Biblio, Mahtma II was the eleventh most frequently encountered god in the past thirty years. Humanity's win-loss ratio was 2-9, or eighteen percent. That was actually a pretty good record compared to humanity's overall performance in the gods' games.

Those two victories, however, had both been achieved with oversized parties—more than thirty apostles each. No matter how far back you looked in the records, no one had ever defeated this deity with fewer than twenty people.

*"The unique spice of this game is in* numbers.*"*

The God of the Sun Army, Mahtma II, commanded innumerable troops, suggesting a preference for what you might call MMT—Massively Multiplayer Tactics.

"I should've known all that. What an idiot I am," said Camilla, leader of Team Archangel. She was at the head of the group of fifteen apostles sprinting across the burning sand. She had to constantly slide her glasses up the bridge of her nose, since they threatened to fall off with every stride. "I only saw the god and three servants. And since we had fifteen people, including Lady Leoleshea, I thought this was going to be an easy win. What a miscalculation!"

The Sunsteal Scramble had started. That pyramid on the horizon seemed impossibly far away, with the desert all around them. Meanwhile, the god's army of 1,667 creatures howled from the dunes behind them and nipped at their heels.

"At this rate, it's nothing but a game of tag!" Camilla complained.

The tan girl, Kelritch, caught up with her from behind. "You're the data-driven type, yet you failed to sufficiently analyze the data available. Having a bit of an identity crisis?"

"Oh, stuff it!"

"One other thing. I'd advise against holding your flower in your hand. You should tuck it into your clothing."

"You just *have* to boss a person around, don't you? ...Not that it's a bad idea."

"If you'll excuse me, then." Kelritch went ahead, all but skipping over the sand, her movements easy and elegant despite the difficult terrain.

Pearl looked positively astounded. "Wow! How can Kelritch go so fast?"

"Amazing what a little confidence will do for a person," Camilla grumbled.

Apostles with Superhuman Arises were blessed with enhanced physical abilities—but the form they took was as diverse as the apostles themselves. Fay, for example, was hardly more capable than an ordinary person off the street, whereas Kelritch truly *looked* superhuman. And she hadn't even activated her Arise yet.

"She might really be helpful to have around. Which means that if *that* goes *there*, the Sun Flower will..."

"What are you muttering about, Fay?" Pearl asked.

"Doing some calculations. Thinking through how things are likely to go from here."

No sooner were the words out of his mouth than there was an earthshaking *boom* that scattered sand into the air.

"Oh! Oh no!" Pearl cried.

"Mrrow!"

"Mrrrr!"

The god's beasts sped up, dust clouds whirling behind them. They looked like adorable stuffed animals—stuffed animals that were two meters long and weighed more than a hundred kilograms. And there were more than a thousand of them. As they came toward the apostles, they created what looked like a tidal wave of dust and sand. It was intimidating, to say the least.

And they were so fast. A second ago they'd been just standing there; now they'd all leapt down from the dunes.

"If we assume it was two hundred meters down the face of the dunes, and it took them twelve seconds to get to the bottom, that would be about sixty kilometers an hour. Yeah, they'll have no problem catching us at that rate," Fay said.

"Please don't make it sound like you're just giving up!" Pearl said.

"Nah. This is about what I expected."

A simple game of tag across the sands was always going to work out in the god's favor. The cat golems would easily catch the humans before they could run all the way to the pyramid. If they couldn't, there was no game here.

"They're rubber-banded—flexible so that they adjust their own abilities depending on ours. If we could run eighty kilometers an hour, they'd be able to do a hundred. The game's just built that way."

"You're not making our chances of winning sound any better!"

"The point of the game is what do we do about it?"

This was the Sunsteal Scramble. In principle, victory could be achieved by racing to the pyramid in the distance. But the god's army was faster than the humans. That was the heart of this game. *They're guaranteed to catch us before we get there. That's a message:* Do something about it. *Using our Arises, or otherwise the mechanics of the game itself.*

The Sun Flower and the Poison Flower, say.

Fay's intuition had told him that a footrace to the pyramid was too simple—it didn't make sense. There had to be something more going on here than a fun run across the desert.

"That'd be too easy for one of the gods' games. If this were a marathon, there'd be checkpoints on the way to the pyramid. Or maybe there are special gimmicks, the sort of tricks you could only pull in a desert."

This was what he knew so far:

**Sunsteal Scramble**
**Win Condition 1: Run to the pyramid and offer the Sun Flower on the highest level.**
**Win Condition 2: Steal the god team's Sun Flower.**
**Lose Condition 1: The human team's Sun Flower is stolen.**
**Rule: If at any time the number of flowers you're carrying is 0, you're out.**
**Relay Checkpoint: ???**

As Fay was thinking everything through, Leshea, who was bringing up the rear of the fifteen-person crew, bellowed: "Hey, human up front!"

Kelritch, leading the way, took a quick glance back at the shouting former god.

"Get outta the way!"

"Wha?!"

"Kelritch, *jump backward!*" Dax shouted.

Without even pausing to ask why, Kelritch kicked off the sand. At the same moment, a beast wearing a pointy hat at the far back of the god's army raised a wand in a sweeping motion, just like a wizard from some old fairy tale. "Time for some divine *purrr*nishment!" the beast said. A dark wind began to blow, spinning up from beneath Kelritch's feet and pulling up the sand all around as it formed a great, black whirlwind.

"A sandstorm?!" Kelritch said, jumping as hard as she could. If it had taken her one second longer, she would have been torn apart by the whirlwind and out of the game.

"N-nobody said there'd be cyclones! If one of those gets you, you're definitely done for!" Pearl said. "And does this mean the cat golems can use ranged magic?!"

They'd been trying to get as much distance on the cat army as they possibly could, thinking that every inch made them safer—but it turned out that wasn't true at all.

*That spell targeted Kelritch—the person right at the front of our formation. It must be "divine punishment" for people who get too far ahead of the pursuers!*

So, get too close and they would catch you—but run outside a specified area of safety, and you'd be beaten back with a powerful blast of magic.

"I don't think a human would stand much chance against one of those," Leshea said, looking at the whirlwind as it stretched into the sky. "You remember the flashes of light that went after anyone who attacked Uroboros's tail? I think it's the same sort of thing."

The god's sandstorm was like a wall, but behind them, Mahtma's soldiers of sand leapt through it, unbothered.

"Mrrah!"

"No! Beasts!"

"Captain, they're gonna catch—aghhh!" A member of Archangel was tackled by one of the creatures. Adorable though they might be, they were still the soldiers of a god, and they hit like it. Even a Superhuman would be hard-pressed to keep their head on their shoulders when one of these cats pounced. And because using magic would hit their friends at this distance, the mages were pinned, too.

"Help! Help meee!"

"You monster! Let him go!" Another apostle gave the golem a whack from behind in an attempt to help their friend, but was rewarded only with a *boosh*, the sand that constituted the beast's body re-formed itself immediately.

"Meow!" the beast said.

"Oh, shit!" the apostle yelled at almost the same time.

In the creature's paw was a flower bud, stolen from an apostle. It opened slowly to reveal petals as white as snow.

*One of the Sand Flowers.* Its loss wouldn't inflict defeat, but the human who had lost it was out of the game.

"Hngh?!" the apostle exclaimed.

Camilla, the apostle's team leader, reached out, but she was too late. The apostle was enveloped in light and shimmered away like a fading mirage.

*That's one down. Fourteen more humans.*

The sand beasts came piling down toward Camilla like an avalanche.

"Why, you—!" she shouted. "So you got one of us—so what?!" Her fingertip began to glow with a blue light. It went flying from her finger, sweeping across the desert accompanied by a blast of cold air worthy of a blizzard. "Frostbite!" she yelled.

A bullet of ice slammed into one of the golems. In the space of an instant, its entire body was encased in ice, turning it into a blue statue. Sand or not, it wouldn't be going anywhere like that.

"How do you like—"

"Mrow!" "Mrow!" "Mrow!" "Mrow!" "Mrow!" "Mrow!" "Mrow!" "Mrow!"

"There's way too many of them!" said Camilla as dozens more cat-soldiers came pouring past their frozen compatriot. The deep freeze wouldn't last forever, and meanwhile Magical Arises had a cooldown time, a specific span before they could be used again. There would be no machine-gunning of ice bullets. "Daaax!" Camilla yelled, calling to the young man in the black coat, who was glaring at the beasts. "This is a race, not a staring contest! You need to move!"

"I see," Dax said with a snorting laugh. Mal-ra's foremost apostle gave a dramatic flourish of his coat. "I'm most interested to see how Fay plays this game, but if my team is in danger, then it's time for some new priorities. Reaching out to a friend in need is part of what makes a game so much f—"

"Just shut up and run!"

"Therefore, O god, O divine army! Behold my power!" He raised his right hand, thrusting it toward the creatures coming on like a wall of sand. "Dax Hurricane!"

For a few brief seconds, Fay completely forgot about the crisis at hand, everything in his mind consumed by one single, overpowering question: *Dax Hurricane?* It reminded him of the card Dax had played in Mind Arena, something to match up against Pearl Fire. Dax Thunder, was that it?

"Hey, uh, Dax, isn't that a sugoroku sp—"

He didn't get to finish. *Fwoom!* A cutting wind sprang up, slicing through the beasts one after another.

"Wait! That's really its name?!"

Dax Gear Scimitar: the Arcane Court's data recorded that he was a superlative user of wind magic. And Fay had seen the data, of course. But the data hadn't mentioned what he called his spell.

"Wow, it's…it's beautiful!" Pearl said, trembling. "As powerful as it is brilliantly named! A girl could get jealous!"

"I don't think now is the time, Pearl! Above you!"

"Eh?" She looked up to discover a lone cat golem that had escaped Dax Hurricane flying through the air. It had sprung off the sand with the sort of agility only a feline possessed. "I—I don't wanna be crushed!" Pearl yelped and scrambled backward, but the sand gave her no purchase, and her attempt to flee yielded only a few dozen centimeters of distance. The beast reached out toward her…

…and dissipated, *bwwsh*. The creature's claws just grazed her, running from her collar down to her shoulder.

"Oh!" she said as the fabric tore, sending pieces flying as far as the buttons on her chest. There under the bright sunlight two mounds the size of ripe coconuts and the deep, dark valley in between were revealed… "Oh noooooooooooooo!" she cried.

"Mrrrow!" echoed the cat golems, and then they pounced on her. They were really just going for the flower she'd hidden on her chest, but the scene looked awfully lurid.

"Pearl, don't tell me you did that on purpose!" Fay said.

"And what purpose would that beee?!" Tears in her eyes, Pearl tried to hold what was left of her shirt to her chest with one hand while she reached toward the sky with the other. "The Wandering!" she called.

A golden warp portal appeared. She scrambled through it,

which would allow her to teleport to another warp portal within a thirty-meter radius. But she'd made one mistake. A miscalculation induced by the shock of her clothing being torn off, true enough—but she'd forgotten that they were surrounded by more than a thousand of the god's troops. No matter where she went, the beasts would be waiting for her.

"Meowr!"

"Oh, hello, Mr. Cat Golem! I didn't expect to see you here," Pearl greeted the creatures on the far side of her warp. The Wandering had a cooldown time proportional to its substantial power—a full thirty seconds. There was no more running away. "H-h-help meee!" Pearl said.

"Mrrrah!" one of the creatures yowled, pinning Pearl's arms behind her back. Her flower peeked out from a newly exposed inner pocket, while Pearl's bra was now visible.

"I'm at the end of my rope in more ways than ooonne!"

"Mrow!" Another beast reached for Pearl's bountiful chest, its eyes gleaming.

"I hate horny cats," said a tan girl who jumped in front of Pearl and sent the beast flying with a punch to its great sandy body.

"Kelritch?!" Pearl exclaimed.

"Stealing the flowers from the beasts is always a possibility, but it looks like it's quicker just to destroy them."

Kelritch Shee's Arise was called Aura Drive. By focusing shock waves into her limbs, she could deliver powerful punches and kicks. It was mostly useful in battle games, but a moment like this was perfect for her to strut her stuff.

"I have a boxing license," Kelritch added.

"Really?!"

"I'm often told it seems out of character."

Just like a boxer in the ring, Kelritch hunched and kept herself covered as she closed in on the beast holding Pearl. It only took her the space of a breath.

"Mrow?!"

"This is goodbye, you filthy feline." She sent the beast flying with an uppercut. It cried "Mrrrahhhh!" as it arced through the air, then returned to dust when it smashed into the ground.

Pearl collapsed to her knees. "Cough... Cough... Th-thank you very much!" Getting back up unsteadily, she said, "I think I'll call that Cosmic Impact!"

"I do not believe I gave it any such name. Since we're on the same team today, it's only natural that I would try to help you. I also simply wanted to eliminate those shameless cats. How dare they manhandle a young lady." Kelritch's face remained completely impassive throughout this speech. Her eyes, however, stopped cold when they reached Pearl's chest. She studied the two generous fruits, which Pearl couldn't hide with one hand even if she tried. And she *was* trying.

"I-is something the matter?" Pearl asked.

"No. Nothing," Kelritch said, turning around as if completely detached. "I shouldn't have saved you."

"What? Why not?!" Pearl cried.

At that moment, there was a shout. Pearl and Kelritch turned toward it to discover that a crowd of the beasts had set upon the members of Team Archangel. They looked like celebrities being swarmed by fans. The creatures threw themselves at the human team members, grabbing their hidden flowers.

"You guys! What's happening?!" Camilla exclaimed, watching the members of her team disappear in flashes of light. The god's troops gave them no time to bemoan their companions but jumped at the next target, kicking up sand as they went.

"Tsk!" Dax sucked his teeth. This was the inherent weakness

of mages—they could unleash powerful spells across large areas, but in a situation like this, they were as likely to hit their friends as their foes. "Camilla, what about your magic?"

"No... I'll never be in time!" Camilla bit her lip. She was still on cooldown. As team leader, she was trying to freeze every beast she could, but powerful magic entailed an equally lengthy cooldown period. "There's just too many of them! At this rate, we—"

"Get down!"

"Wha—?"

"Everyone still standing, hit the sand and brace yourselves for a shock wave!" Fay shouted. He saw the vermilion-haired girl at the tail end of their formation—her eyes were shining, and she looked restless.

"Guess we're running low on options," they could hear her say. An adorable fang could be seen in a corner of her mouth. "I don't like resorting to force, but with the opponent having so many more pieces than we do, well, there's not much choice. Man, I really don't like having to get violent."

*That* was a dirty, rotten lie. Fay knew it, Pearl knew it, and quite a bit farther away, Ruin's Chief Secretary Miranda knew it.

Leshea said simply, "*Shatter.*"

The Dragon God Leoleshea slammed her fist into the ground, and the ocean of sand split in two.

There was a quaking that threatened to turn the whole world upside down, and then a shock wave that could easily have collapsed a building traveled all the way to the horizon.

"Mrow?!" "Mr-mr-mrrrw!"

A vast crevasse opened, a bottomless pit that swallowed the cat golems by the hundreds.

"All right, let's get a move on!" said Leshea. She set off running as if nothing had happened. As if she *hadn't* just opened a kilometers-long rent in the earth with her fist.

"I have a feeling that if we made her angry, it might just mean the end of the human world," Kelritch said in amazement.

"Shh," Fay said. "She'll hear you." Then he went running after the former goddess. "Be careful, Leshea! You'll be in trouble if you get too far away from the beasts!"

"You mean that 'divine punishment'?" She slowed down a little bit, matching pace with Fay and Pearl and the seven other remaining humans. "Come with me. That pit won't last forever."

"Hrg... You heard her. Let's go, everyone!" Camilla shouted to her four surviving teammates. They were all covered in sand and looking much worse for wear after being attacked by the beasts.

So, there were ten people left on the human team. Fay heard roaring behind them and looked back to see the hole Leshea had made closing itself up even as he watched.

*Just like she said. This is Mahtma II's personal Elements. I'm sure the god can fix up the desert as often as necessary.*

The beasts were starting to jump over the rift. The race to the pyramid was on again...or so Fay thought.

"Huh?" said Camilla, who was running at the front of the group.

"What's that?" added Leshea, who was next to her.

Fay looked ahead again and saw that as they ran, the shimmering heat haze in the air gave way, revealing something they hadn't been able to see before: a verdant strip of green land right in the middle of the desert.

"Is that a forest?" Leshea pondered.

"N-no, Lady Leoleshea—it's an oasis!" Camilla said. An area of dense vegetation made possible by water underground. This desert, though, had been crafted by Mahtma II for the purposes of this game. The oasis had to hide some trick as well.

"Hmph. Here I thought we were in for a simple footrace, but this desert has a few tricks up its sleeve," Dax muttered. "Kelritch, what do we do about that?"

"We should consider the possibility that it's a trap," she replied immediately. "Our goal is the pyramid, beyond the oasis. Stopping here would be a waste of time at best. I say we simply ignore it and—"

"*Hellooo everyone! I've been waiting for you!*" From amidst the greenery of the oasis emerged the meep. "*Welcome to the relay checkpoint! This is a place for the human team to rest, a safe zone where the beasts won't find you.*"

"Not necessary," Kelritch said flatly. "I'm making for that pyramid, and I'm not stopping. Good day."

"*Oh! There's something I failed to mention,*" the meep said, clapping its hands. "*This game has a hidden mechanic, the Heat Gauge. A little something to make this contest even more heart-racing!*"

They looked at the meep, puzzled.

"*The gauge fills as you endure the pounding desert sun. It reaches maximum if you spend more than twenty consecutive minutes exposed to the elements. And as you've all been out there for eighteen minutes already...*"

"What happens when the gauge maxes out?" Pearl asked.

"*Instant death! Game over!*" the meep replied.

"You couldn't have mentioned that before the game started?!"

"*Well, then it wouldn't have been a hidden mechanic.*"

Faces paled all around as it sank in that they had two minutes until it was game over for all of them. The ten of them, including Fay, rushed into the oasis as fast as they could.

It was like a paradise, green everywhere he looked. With

the first step he took into the oasis, Fay could feel a cool breeze wafting across the nape of his neck. It seemed to take the fever straight out of him. *Didn't realize I'd gotten so overheated*, he thought. *The meep wasn't messing around about that heat gauge.*

The island of greenery was stunning. Flowers of every color bloomed beneath palm trees, and somewhere up ahead they could hear coursing water.

"It really does seem to be a place we can take a break," Pearl said, gazing around but not looking completely convinced. She'd tied the ends of her torn shirt at her shoulder, the improvised solution just managing to hide her bosom.

"Look at that, Fay!" Leshea said, pointing at the god's troops. They were coming across the dunes, but the moment Fay and the others entered the oasis, the beasts started looking around in confusion. You could almost see the question marks over their heads.

"Maybe we really will be able to collect ourselves here," Fay said.

"Um, Fay," Pearl said hesitantly. "Do you still think we can stick to the original plan? We're about halfway to the pyramid, right? But we've taken some losses. Our fifteen apostles are down to ten..."

"I do think this calls for a slight adjustment to *our* strategy."

"Only a slight adjustment?"

"Yeah. In this game, as long as we can avoid our Sun Flower getting stolen, we can pull out a victory somehow. You're right, we've lost some of our teammates, but their sacrifice allowed us to get this far."

Fay was going to continue to expound, but Pearl stuck her hand in the air and cried, "Oh! I thought of a great little trick! As I think you know, Fay, I have a power that I haven't yet used in this game."

"You mean Shift Change?" he said.

Pearl had two teleportation abilities. One was the simple Teleport, which she'd already demonstrated in this match, but the other was called Shift Change. It could swap the positions of any two people or objects Pearl had touched within the past three minutes. Once upon a time, she'd activated it without meaning to and accidentally caused her team to lose a game—but such mistakes notwithstanding, the power was actually a pretty major one.

"If it looks like the person with the Sun Flower is going to be captured, I can use Shift Change to switch it with another flower in an instant! The only constraint is, they have to be within thirty meters of me."

"Yeah, it crossed my mind..." Fay was quiet for a moment, then he said, "Suppose I had the Sun Flower. You're saying you could swap the flower I was carrying and the one you're carrying in the blink of an eye, right?"

"Yep!"

Fay was quiet again. That *was* a powerful ability—a serious card to have in their hand if it looked like they were going to lose their Sun Flower. But there was a catch.

"Pearl... Any chance you think that would invoke the situation the meep warned us about before the game?"

*"Once the game starts, if there's even an instant when you're not carrying a flower, you're considered to have lost your flower and you're out on the spot."*

"I'm worried about 'an instant.' I think if you were to use Shift Change on my flower and yours, for example, there would have to be an instant when the flowers had disappeared from both our hands."

"Oh no!"

"I think it would be pretty risky to try it."

"Yeah... You're right." Pearl's shoulders slumped. "Here I thought I'd had a stroke of genius. But it was a dumb idea."

"No, it actually helps. We should always be on the lookout for more options, and anyway, I was thinking along the same li—"

He was interrupted: *"All right, everyone! Time to rehydrate!"* Ten-ish meeps appeared from the underbrush, hugging small bottles. *"We're here to offer a special drink to those of you lucky enough to have found this oasis. When you drink it, it keeps the heat gauge from filling. We've got honey juice, coconut juice, apple juice, orange juice, and water. Pick whichever one you like!"*

"I want honey juice!" Pearl cried without a second thought. She popped the lid on her bottle and took an eager sip. "Th-this is delicious!" she said, her eyes going wide. "Mellow and rich at the same time, but not too sweet... It goes down so easy! You made this with clover honey, didn't you?"

*"Bingo!"* said the meep.

Behind Pearl, Kelritch was contemplating the meeps' bottles carefully. "Coconut juice... But... Hmm. It's hard to ignore apple juice, the king of juices. Yet we have personal testimony that the honey juice is excellent. I should take that into account. Dax, what are you having?"

"Protein juice," he replied.

*"We don't have that!"* the meep said.

"What?! And why in the world not?"

*"Just didn't think of it."*

"Very well then. I'll have apple juice. Truly, apples are fit to be the fastest and indeed best way to get juice." It was clear that Dax wasn't a man to compromise even when it came to his choice of juice.

Elsewhere, there was a girl studying one of the meeps' bottles even more intently than Dax and Kelritch.

"Whatcha thinkin', Leshea?"

"Just wondering, Fay. Do you think we *have* to drink this?" She was holding a bottle of coconut juice, but sounded uncharacteristically withdrawn for a former god who normally burst with curiosity about every kind of game.

"Hmmm... I guess you don't have to force yourself if they don't have something you like."

"I don't need to eat or drink at all."

"Oh yeah."

Leshea's physical body was one created by a god specifically to play games. She could go for centuries without eating or drinking—she could just keep playing. In fact, Leshea had never had a drink at all.

"Logically speaking, I should be just fine. Putting a tiny bottle of liquid like this into my body wouldn't make any difference, anyway." Leshea gave the bottle a look as if it were odd to her, a bit like a kitten seeing a puddle for the first time. Slowly, hesitantly, she brought it to her lips and took a sip.

"Pbbbbt!" She spat it right back out. She could only have sipped a few milliliters—was a spit take that big really necessary?

"Geez! You'll get it all over me!" Fay said.

"I can't do it! It's not possible!" Leshea shook her head vigorously. "My body is rejecting this impure stuff!"

"It's not... Well, I mean, I guess it sort of is." At least, it probably was for the body of a god. For a perfect body that never needed to rehydrate, something like this was simply superfluous. "Don't worry about it. It's not a big deal," Fay said.

"It is." Leshea bit her lip, frustrated. "As a player, it's only polite to get through all the tricks and gimmicks in a game!"

"Okay, so what are you going to do?"

There was a beat, then Leshea held the bottle out toward Fay. "I'll let you do it."

"You want me to drink it?"

"No!"

"What, then?"

"Fay..." He'd never heard her sound so feeble. She stared straight at him, her eyes brimming with tears. "Help me drink it. Force me."

Any response stuck in Fay's throat.

"I'm just...not used to this sort of thing." Her eyes were as beautiful as gemstones. "Please?"

"Nuh-uh. No way."

"Why not?!"

"Because it would be...uh, *awkward*, is maybe the word I'd choose. Anyway, if you can't drink it, just get rid of it." Fay heaved a sigh. Then he noticed Pearl; she of the honey juice. He beckoned her over, then lowered his voice to make sure the meep couldn't hear him. "Say, Pearl, there was something important I wanted to talk to you about. Don't tell anyone else."

"What is it?" Pearl asked.

*"Leshea isn't the one with the Sun Flower."*

"What?!" The golden-haired girl practically rose off the ground with shock. "Wh-wh-why not?! I mean! Ohh! The way both of you said...what you said...at the beginning of the game! But then if Leshea doesn't..."

"Right. You see how it is. Welp, I'm counting on you!" Fay said, and then he spun on his heel and walked away.

Leshea was heaving the mother of all sighs, but the bottle she held was empty.

"Wait, you finished it?" Fay asked.

"I threw it away in the bushes over there," she said, deeply

dejected. "To think—*me*, of all people, giving up on a game mechanic!"

At that moment, a shrill *brrriiiing!* sounded around the oasis, like an alarm clock.

"Wh-what's that?! That sound!" shouted Camilla, jogging back from where she'd been investigating the water source. "Did somebody do something? And what was it?!"

*"Heyo! I forgot one little detail,"* the meep said, drifting down out of the sky. *"Once everyone's drunk their juice, your break in the oasis is over. You're about to find yourselves forcibly ejected."*

"You *really* need to tell us these things sooner!" Pearl said. Then Fay and the others did indeed discover they were being forced out of the oasis as if shoved by an invisible hand. Out in the vast desert under the pounding sun, they promptly started sweating again. "Oh! It looks like we can't go back to the oasis anymore, Fay!" Pearl said, pressing her hand against an invisible wall. Evidently that place of safety was only offered once per game. And meanwhile...

"Mrow!"

"Mrow!" "Mrow!" "Mrow!" "Mrow!"

The beasts were yowling—they must have picked up the humans' scent. Every cat golem on every dune, more than a thousand of them, turned toward the players at the same time.

"They found us! Everyone, make for the pyramid!" Camilla said, pointing at the huge structure.

They all started running, but so did the beasts, and the pursuers were audibly gaining ground. Their footsteps sounded louder and more powerful than before.

"I-is it just me, Fay, or have the cat golems gotten faster?!" Pearl said. The oasis was the halfway point, and past it the game got harder; the god's troops became quicker and their numbers increased.

"This way, Pearl!"

"W-wait up! Please!" she said. She scrambled to create a warp portal—she was the slowest runner among them, and it was all she could do to keep up with Fay and the others even by teleporting thirty meters at a time.

*I'd really prefer to save Pearl's teleportation to get out of an emergency situation, but I guess we don't have that luxury.*

The beasts were coming after them like an avalanche; even Fay felt the hair on the back of his neck stand up knowing they were there. The apostles couldn't escape. Even the beasts who had been on the far horizon were practically breathing down their necks now.

"Leshea! Can you do that thing again?"

"I just need to make a little hole, right?"

Her fist hit the ground. Just like before, there was a dizzying quake, and a tremendous crevasse opened in the desert floor. Confronted with this obstacle...

...the cats picked up speed. Forget screeching to a halt—they ran *faster* as they approached the rift.

"Mrow!"

They took a running leap and vaulted the veritable canyon Leshea had made.

"You've got to be kidding me!" she said. Even she hadn't expected this. She jumped backward herself as hundreds of the beasts landed on the apostles' side of the divide. She was being careful—the god's troops might have more tricks up their sleeve, and she'd decided not to engage them directly until she knew for sure what they were hiding.

They could hear Mahtma's voice resounding across the desert: *"Forward, my army!"* The cats charged.

"Crap! Get outta the way!" One of the other apostles thrust his hand out, and sparks of flame gathered in his palm, forming a bullet of fire that he unleashed at the oncoming cat golems.

*Bwwshh!*

The fire…simply dissipated, absorbed by a sand shield the beasts raised as one.

"They have a magic-proof shield?!" the apostle howled.

"*Purrrsue them!*" the cats could be heard saying. "*Remeowve their flowers!*" Dozens of the sand creatures fell upon the apostles of Archangel, who threw themselves on the ground. They dropped out as the cats took their flowers, returned one by one from the desert to the real world.

"Hey! No! Get your paws off me, you—!" Camilla, Archangel's bespectacled team leader, was struggling with a beast who had her by the collar. By the time Fay and the others turned toward her, several of the creatures already had her pinned.

"Camilla!" Pearl said, reaching out, but the other woman shouted, "Stay back!" Pearl flinched, intimidated by the horrendous look Camilla was giving her.

"I have a Sand Flower!" Camilla said. "It won't matter if they take it!"

"Y-yeah, but…"

"Run for the pyramid! As for you, you gropey golems, you're gonna be sorry you ever grabbed me!" Both her hands glowed blue. "Freeze, felines!"

Ice Wall: the beasts that had been about to jump at Fay and the remaining apostles slammed into a wall of ice that burst from the ground. It was a good old-fashioned physical obstacle. No matter how magic-proof their shield might be, it was no help against the towering frozen barrier.

"Don't worry about us, just go!" Camilla cried from where she and Archangel were trapped on the cat-golem side of the wall.

"All right… I'm sorry!" Fay called back, and then he spun and ran. He guessed they had about six hundred meters to go to the pyramid, the gigantic triangular structure obviously getting closer even to the naked eye.

> Five humans remaining. (1 Sun Flower, 1 Poison Flower, 3 Sand Flowers.)
> 1,987 god's team members remaining including Mahtma II. (1 Sun Flower, 1 Poison Flower, 1,985 Sand Flowers.)

"We're pressing on!" said Dax, who went to the head of the human group. His black coat billowed as he worked his way along the sand, clutching his flower in his hand.

Kelritch wasn't far behind him. "Dax, don't you think you should hide your flower?"

"If they get their hands on me, it'll be over anyway. If hiding it won't do any good, I might as well have it ready to throw if the need arises."

"Good thinking," the tanned girl said with a sound of admiration. "We've got about five hundred meters to the pyramid. If I had the Sun Flower, I think this is when I would start running as hard as I could."

"Are you saying you don't?"

"What about you, Dax?"

"Mine's Sand. Let them take it; it won't make a difference."

"I see..." Kelritch looked over her shoulder. She knew, then, that either Fay, Leshea, or Pearl must have the Sun Flower.

It was then, in that split second of inattention, that the sand under her feet began to shift. She could hear it, a sort of scratching sound. She'd left an opening.

"Wha?!"

One of the beasts lunged out from under the sand. Had it

been hiding there, or was it freshly created? Whichever, it caught Kelritch unawares—she'd been assuming the creatures still had some distance to cover before they could get her—and her reaction was a fraction too slow.

"Mrah!" the golem yowled.

"Dax Wind!" It was Dax's wind magic. He crafted as delicate a whirlwind as he could and sent the golem flying as it tried to attack Kelritch.

Far away on the horizon, though, Fay saw a beast with a big, pointy hat raise its staff. "Divine *purrr*nishment!" it called.

Kelritch paled as she realized the god's judgment was about to fall upon the black-coated young man. "Dax?!"

"O-oh no you don't! The Wandering!" Pearl shouted. A golden portal appeared in front of Dax. "Dax, jump in!" she cried. It was the one way he could escape the maelstrom. Dax rushed for the portal, the tips of his fingers brushing the golden ring...

...and then the god's sandstorm swallowed him up.

"Daaax!" Fay shouted. The storm seemed powerful enough to tear the very sky asunder. It could certainly force a player out. Dax might be Mal-ra's most revered apostle, but he was still only human. No one could survive an attack like that.

Dax Gear Scimitar was out of the game. The human team was down to just four people—Fay, Leshea, Pearl, and Kelritch.

A cry of "You...damn...sand monsterrr!" rent the air, and Kelritch went racing toward the wizard-like golem—the exact opposite direction from the pyramid.

"Kelritch, wait!" Fay shouted.

But she said, "I'm of perfectly sound mind, Fay." She never even turned around, just kept running. "You of all people ought to know—I'm holding a Sand Flower." She raised her fist. "Fay,

Pearl. Lady Leoleshea. One of you three must have the Sun Flower. Which means the most help I can give right now is to slow them down. Now that we've been reduced to four players, the only thing to do is to try to reach that pyramid as fast as humanly possible."

"I like the way you think," Leshea said.

"What?"

"I'm not carrying the Sun Flower, either. So maybe I'll just go with you."

There was a hiss of sand as Leshea leapt to join Kelritch and they charged toward the god's army.

———————

The Dive Center in the Arcane Court Mal-ra branch office was so silent that you could even hear dust settling. No one said a word. They forgot to breathe as they stared at the screen. The tension was absolute.

Until it was broken by someone tumbling into the room with an "Ow, that hurts!" A female apostle came sliding out of the Undine statue's water jug. "The gods sure don't have much mercy on people who go out of a game, do they?"

The girl who had emerged from the statue had wavy brown hair, and her glasses had gone askew with the force of her landing. She straightened them, then looked around at everyone in the room. "I can only apologize, Chief Secretary," she said.

"Not at all. You did well, Camilla." The chief secretary with his craggy face and sunglasses nodded at her from where he sat on a tube-frame chair.

Players who went out of the gods' games were returned to the real world. With Camilla's arrival, all ten members of Team Archangel were back.

"I've got a question, Camilla," the chief secretary said to the recently returned apostle. "We can all see that the odds aren't looking good in this game. There are four humans left against a divine force of at least a thousand, maybe two."

"Yes, sir."

"We want to know: Who has the Sun Flower?"

Silence returned to the room. Every one of the tens of thousands of viewers probably had the exact same question at that moment.

"I'm afraid I just don't know, sir," Camilla replied with a weak smile and a shrug. "Fay was the one who handed out the flowers—none of us knew who had what. At least now we can be sure that it was all Sand Flowers for Archangel."

"So the Sun and Poison Flowers are both still out there?"

"Yes, sir... But practically speaking, I think only one of two people can be carrying the Sun Flower." Camilla turned to the big screen, and the people currently on it. "This game is about getting the Sun Flower to the pyramid—but Lady Leoleshea and Kelritch have both given up trying to get there in favor of slowing down the enemy. I think that makes it clear that neither of them has the Sun Flower."

"Yes, it would have to be one of the two who're still heading for the goal," the chief secretary said quietly. "Meaning Fay or Pearl. And if one of them has the Sun Flower, I think it's fair to assume the other one has the Poison Flower."

> Fay: Sun or Poison Flower. (Going for the pyramid.)
> Pearl: Sun or Poison Flower. (Going for the pyramid.)
> Dragon God Leoleshea: Sand Flower. (Not going for the pyramid, but slowing down the enemy.)
> Kelritch: Sand Flower. (Not going for the pyramid, but slowing down the enemy.)

So anyone could see this was the case. If there was a problem, it was that this fact would be just as obvious to the god Mahtma II as it was to any of the rest of them.

That was when there was the distinct *tap* of a firm footfall sounding through the room.

"Dax?!"

The black-coated young man came out of the statue, landing nimbly on his feet. Everyone in the Dive Center stared at him. "Nel," he said. She sucked in her breath and met his eyes. She'd been standing on the sidelines in the room, trying to stay quiet. "I've done what I owed you under our wager," Dax said.

Namely, the one they'd made two days earlier, right here in this building.

*"There's a friendly little match planned for tomorrow—my team versus his. If I should happen to lose, I'll do any one thing you ask. Anything at all. But if and when I defeat Fay..."*

*"Then you want me to join your team."*

Fay had won the "friendly match," unknowingly earning Nel the right to demand something of Dax.

"'Do everything in your power to help Fay achieve victory.' That's what you asked for, was it not?"

"Yes... It was."

"I think we're about to witness the endgame," Dax said, looking very self-assured for someone who'd just retired from a game. "Just watch. Let's see how the man you've chosen plays."

# 2

The heat wafted from the desert. Kelritch all but tumbled down the dunes as she fled from dozens of sand golems as fast as she could.

"Mrow!" the golems cried.

"They don't know when to give up!" Kelritch *tsk*ed. She could feel them behind her; she couldn't seem to shake them. Even with her Superhuman speed, she couldn't lose them—if anything, they kept getting closer. Maybe she shouldn't have been surprised: the god's beasts got faster and faster as time passed in the game. "Quick! We said we'd buy time, but we're not going to buy much at this rate!"

Breathing hard, Kelritch looked toward the two people in the distance, making for the pyramid.

The four-sided structure shimmered golden ahead of them, the sunlight glinting off of it. "Huff! Huff... Fay, we're almost there!" Pearl yelled, pointing.

They'd made it. They'd reached the ancient tomb of piled stones. Leshea and Kelritch were holding off the thousands of beasts as best they could—this was Fay and Pearl's opportunity to make for the top of the pyramid.

"I'm sure you realize this by now, Pearl, but just to be completely clear..." Fay, his breath ragged, took out the flower he'd been hiding near his chest. "...I've got the Sun Flower!"

It wasn't Leshea or even Kelritch, the two strongest and most obvious candidates, who had the Sun Flower. Instead, Fay had kept it for himself.

"If we get this thing to the top of that pyramid, we win!"

"R-right! I'll protect you with everything I've got!"

On the front face of the pyramid, built into the piles of blocks that formed the structure, was—not a staircase, but a massive slope that led directly to the top. Fay just needed to get up it...

*"Well done making it this far."*

The stern telepathic voice of Mahtma II reached them from far overhead. There was a scraping sound like armor rasping, and the god itself walked slowly down the slope from the top of the pyramid. *"Now show me how you will ascend this path."*

Mahtma held its staff high with both hands, a gesture so intimidating that Fay and Pearl both broke out in a cold sweat. They'd outwitted and outrun thousands of Mahtma's servants to get here, but the deity had a sheer, inescapable presence unlike that of any of the beasts.

"Fay?!" Pearl said.

"Don't stop, Pearl. We've got one place to be, and Mahtma's in our way!"

What else could he say? The god stood like an insuperable wall between them and the summit—but if they didn't get up that pyramid, there would be no victory.

*But how are we supposed to do that without Leshea?! We're not going to beat a god by force. We'll have to gamble everything on Pearl's Arise.* Teleportation could get them past the god. If they could wait until they were within arm's reach of Mahtma, a thirty-meter warp could put them near the top of the pyramid.

For one instant, Fay focused all his attention and concentration on forming that idea—and Mahtma saw it. *"Come to me, my army. Summon Cats!"*

"Huh?!" The sand by Fay's feet started to squirm, grains flying upward and grabbing onto his legs.

*"I've got you meow!"*

Huge forms began to emerge from the sand. One had Fay's

ankle, but more of them were appearing, catching first his left arm, then his thigh in viselike grips. He couldn't move, let alone escape.

"Fay?!" Pearl cried.

"Forget about me!" With his last free limb, his right arm, he flung his flower to her. The white bud arced through the air. The second it reached Pearl's hands, Mahtma II and all the cat golems that had been restraining Fay turned their attention to Pearl.

*"The Sun?!"*

If it was just a Sand Flower—there would be no point in throwing it to her—while if Fay had the Poison Flower, he would have simply let Mahtma's troops take it. The fact that he had given his flower to Pearl could only mean one thing.

*Pearl confirmed to have the Sun Flower. (She also has one other flower, either Sand or Poison.)*

"Pearl! It's all down to your Teleport now! Run for it!"

No sooner were the words out of Fay's mouth than the god ordered all the golems: *"Catch her!"*

The beasts holding the now flowerless Fay flung him down and began chasing Pearl up the slope. Mahtma waited ahead of her; the beasts were closing in behind. A pincer movement.

"This is perfect!" Pearl said. She clutched the flower Fay had given her and powered up the slope.

*"You think you can get past me?"* Mahtma said.

"I'd better if I want to get to the very top!"

If she slowed down, the golems would catch her. Pearl focused everything on the god ahead of her, who stood with staff raised and arms wide. Her breath came in great gulps as she climbed. She was ten meters from Mahtma. Then eight. Then five.

God and human acted at the same moment.

*"You are in the divine presence."*

"The Wandering!"

Mahtma II reached out, but the instant before the god could grab her, Pearl jumped into a glowing golden warp portal.

*"Hoh..."*

Mahtma was a god, one of those who bestowed Arises upon humans. As a player in the gods' games, this would not be the first time the deity had encountered a Teleporter. It was all too obvious what this human was up to. She hoped to leap past the god to reach the top of the pyramid.

*"I have you now."* Mahtma turned, staff high, toward the slope to the summit, to find the golden-haired girl......not there. *"Hrm?"*

Where could she be? She was nowhere on the slope. Instantaneous or not, there were limits to teleportation. Where could she have—

"I'm up here!" came a voice—from thirty meters overhead. She hadn't teleported toward the top of the pyramid at all. Mahtma had turned around on the assumption that was exactly what Pearl would do, but instead she was directly above the god. "There's two ways we humans can win this!"

**Win Condition 1: Run to the pyramid and offer the Sun Flower on the highest level.**
**Win Condition 2: Steal the god team's Sun Flower.**

She was aiming for the staff Mahtma II carried. Specifically, for the glass bulb on the end with the flower inside. For the very god to carry it, it could only be the Sun Flower.

Mahtma was an instant late in responding to Pearl's air ambush.

"If we get that flower, victory is ours!" Pearl said. She formed a fist as she dropped and smashed the bulb on Mahtma's staff with unerring accuracy. There was a clear ringing of breaking glass, the shards flying everywhere. The flower, freed from its glass shell, fell neatly into Pearl's palm. "Did... Did I do it?!" she said. "I did it!" She thrust the bud to the heavens, jumping up with excitement. "Fay, I did it! I got the god's flower, everyone!"

The bud slowly opened, revealing the flower within.

The ominous black flower.

"Um. Um?"

No sooner had the sound of confusion escaped Pearl's mouth than she froze, as if her entire body were chained in place. A five-second stun: the debuff, the divine punishment, prescribed for the team that stole the Poison Flower.

"No... Why?"

"*You humans staked your hopes on the belief that I myself would have the Sun Flower, yes?*" Mahtma II said, approaching the immobilized Pearl step by step, in no hurry at all.

No... Pearl realized she could feel, ever so faintly, a cold tremor of disquiet. This was supposed to be a battle of wits—so what if even the possibility that the god was carrying the Sun Flower was itself a trap? Mahtma II had of course never said a word about having the flower. It had simply been a fond human hope.

"But... But..."

"*You wish to know where my team's Sun Flower is? As a special act of favor, I shall tell you.*"

The god gestured toward the desert that spread out beneath them. On the horizon, Pearl saw a golden glimmer like the sun reflecting in the sky. It turned out no member of Mahtma's army had the Sun Flower—there wasn't a single golem near the flash

Pearl saw. But there were palm trees, and bushes, and copious plant life...

"You must be joking!" she exclaimed.

*"Do you humans not say, where better to hide a tree than in the forest?"*

It was none other than the relay checkpoint, the place of rest to which the meep had invited the human team.

The god's Sun Flower was concealed among the others blossoming in the oasis.

Pearl remembered something—before the game had started, the meep had said, *"The god who is my master will appear when your strategy meeting is over."*

Meaning it took time for the god to come to them. At that very moment, Mahtma must have been hiding the Sun Flower in the oasis. Then the god must have claimed the Poison Flower from whichever golem had it and put it in the staff.

It had all meant something. Even the very fact that it had taken Mahtma time to appear had been a hint from the god at the right strategy. *The oasis itself was one way of clearing the game.* It was odd—yes, outrageous. Putting the Sun Flower right where not only Pearl but all the spectators around the world could see it! Yet not a single human had outwitted this god.

They'd been put in their place. After the Giant God Titan and the Endless God Uroboros, a naive belief had begun to take root, an idea that maybe, just maybe, they could win this one too. Well, any such pride or ambition had been shattered. The gods were not so soft. The humans had used every ounce of wit, thought ahead as far as they could, played every mind game that was available to them—and still they hadn't bested their opponent. That was what made Mahtma a god.

*"The Poison Flower's effects will reveal the location of your own Sun Flower. Not that it could be with anyone but you,"* Mahtma said.

It was all Pearl could do to breathe as the two flowers tumbled from her paralyzed hand. One bud hit the ground, slowly opening under Mahtma II's watchful gaze. It was pure white.

*"The first is Sand. It might have been interesting had it been the Poison Flower."*

Then came the second flower, the one Fay had entrusted to Pearl, the one she had vowed to defend with her life. The god plucked it up and it slowly opened.

*"This game is finished…"*

The bud revealed a pure white flower.

*"What?!"*

"What?" Even Pearl was brought up short when she saw the color of the flower that bloomed at her feet. She'd been so sure that Fay had given her the Sun Flower—but this was a Sand Flower. "B-but how?! Why?!"

Pearl herself was out of the game now that her flowers had been taken from her. In the instant before she was returned to the real world, though, she thought she would see where her team's Sun Flower was, its location revealed by the effect of the Poison Flower. But off on the horizon, neither Leshea's nor Kelritch's flowers reacted. They were the only human team members left.

*No one has our Sun Flower,* Pearl realized.

"Why?" The god's telepathy sounded staticky. When Pearl thought about it, she realized she'd felt it all along. From the moment Fay and Leshea had made the pronouncements that had startled viewers all around the world. She'd had a sense that something was going to happen.

*        *        *

*"I've got the Sun Flower!"* they'd both said.

They'd been offering a challenge to the god. At that moment, Mahtma or anyone watching around the world should have been able to parse the possibilities, if they could stay calm enough:

> Possibility 1: Fay was lying, and Leshea had the Sun Flower.
> Possibility 2: Leshea was lying, and Fay had the Sun Flower.
> Possibility 3: Fay and Leshea were both lying, and one of
> the remaining 13 apostles had the Sun Flower.

But the truth lay in…

Possibility 4: No one had the Sun Flower.

It shouldn't have been possible. That much was obvious from a quick review of what had happened so far.

1. Before the start of the game, the meep had given a flower to each of them. (Pearl herself had the Sun Flower in the initial distribution.)
2. Fay had collected all 15 flowers and redistributed them.
3. After 2, it was certain that *someone* on the human team had the Sun Flower. It must have been with one of them. Yet neither one of the remaining human players had it.

*"What in the world is going on?"* Mahtma said. The desert began to quake, Mahtma II's rage echoing through the endless world of sand with something akin to a furious yell. *"Where has the Sun gone?!"*

It was at that moment that they heard a voice. Clear, unmistakable—the voice of a boy who should no longer have been there.

"I'll tell you. Time to compare answers, 'O god'!"

That voice. That young man. The very god, along with viewers all over the world, could hardly believe what they were seeing. Why wasn't he out? He'd tossed his flower to Pearl!

"Fay?!" Kelritch was just as surprised as the rest of them to see him jogging across the desert.

It was an incredible move, an unbelievable play. Not just that he was still there, but that in his hand shone the Sun Flower.

"It's simple," Fay said, looking up at the towering pyramid as he worked his way across the vast field of sand. "I've had two flowers all along."

Mahtma II made a sound of astonishment, for in that moment it all made sense.

> Fay: Had a Sun Flower and a Sand Flower; threw the
> Sand Flower to Pearl.

Fay had two flowers—a simple trick to make the god think he'd thrown Pearl the Sun Flower. Without his flower, Fay was out of the game—which caused Mahtma to ignore him and pursue Pearl, who presumably had the Sun Flower. Everything was just as Fay had planned.

"You're probably wondering how I had two flowers," Fay said, speaking not to the god, but to everyone watching the battle. "Don't you remember? There was one apostle who went out *even though the beasts never got him.*"

*"Hmph. What a ridiculous farce."*

\* \* \*

Fay almost thought he could see the black-coated apostle's smirk as he watched everything unfold from far, far away. Dax had been taken out by the divine sandstorm. It was exactly what he'd been looking for: the most natural way to get out of the game without having his flower stolen. Instead, at that exact moment...

*"The Wandering! Dax, jump in!"*
*Dax rushed for the portal, the tips of his fingers brushing the golden ring...*

And as they'd brushed its surface, Dax had flung his flower into the warp portal, giving it to Fay. It wouldn't have been possible if he'd only thought of it on the spot. But he hadn't.

*"Dax, don't you think you should hide your flower?"*
*"I might as well have it ready to throw if the need arises."*

It had been his plan all along. By getting himself caught up in the sandstorm, Dax could hide the moment at which he gave Fay his flower. But as for Mahtma (and perhaps the entire human world), they believed that the sandstorm had swallowed Dax, flower and all. They never dreamed that he'd given the Sun Flower to Fay.

"The gods smile on those who make their own miracles," Fay said. "How about it? It was a fun game, right, deity?"

*"Most delightful!"* Mahtma II could be heard laughing loud and long, then spread its arms wide. The slope to the top of the pyramid—to the altar abutting the heavens—was blocked by this massive god. *"The path to the sun stands before you. Tread it, if you can!"*

This was single combat: if Fay could reach the altar, he would be victorious. But he would literally have to surpass the god to do it.

"*Come to me, my army. Summon Cats!*" Mahtma said, and made to bring the staff down...but then stopped. "*What?*"

Mahtma's staff didn't move. The all-powerful god stood frozen. The very ruler of this gamespace was unable to exercise any power at all.

"*What is this? What's happening?*" Mahtma demanded, but it was all too clear: a five-second stun—the punishment inflicted upon a team that stole the Poison Flower. Unbelievable, but true.

"You, my friend, should have stopped your troops," said a young woman.

Standing there in the desert upon which the pyramid looked down, with her vermilion hair billowing, the former god turned in the sunlight. "The moment you knew neither Fay nor Pearl had the Poison Flower, you should have issued an emergency halt to all three thousand of your soldiers. Who could have the Poison Flower, I wonder!"

"*Grrr!*"

"I made *sure* your troops took it!" In front of Leshea stood a golem with the black Poison Flower in its paw. Right where Leshea had been sure to put it. "I had the Poison Flower—not to throw you off the scent of our Sun Flower, but so I could inflict a stun anytime!"

The Dragon God Leoleshea would never have her flower stolen—and meanwhile, she was powerful enough to force her flower on the enemy at the most opportune moment. It was the exact opposite of the game's obvious credo, that you must never let your flower be taken. Turn that idea on its head, and the humans could force a five-second stun on the god's team at any time.

That had been Leshea's job.

"*But five seconds...!*" Mahtma said. Fay was still at the bottom of the pyramid. The god would regain mobility before Fay reached the top.

"You're thinking it's *just* five seconds, right?" Fay said as he raced toward Mahtma. He pointed boldly at the paralyzed deity. "You're forgetting one very important thing!"

"*And what is that?*"

"Me! I know I'm just an insignificant human from your perspective, but do me a favor and don't let me go slipping your mind!" A tanned girl came rushing up the slope after Fay—her Arise, Aura Drive, in full swing. Her fist might have been small, but its impact could be enormous. "Catapulting Fay to the altar is no trouble at all for me."

"*Grrrrrr!*"

"Now, jump!" Kelritch said, and Fay jumped. Even with all the momentum of his running start, he only made it about two meters into the air.

"That's a pitiful jump. And you call yourself Superhuman?" Kelritch said.

"That's what you're here for!" Fay replied.

"I must admit, Fay, I am the slightest bit jealous of you." Kelritch placed her fist against the bottom of his foot. For the briefest second, her ever-impassive face displayed a very small but unmistakable smile. "Ever since you arrived, Dax has thought only of you."

"I'm sorry, what?"

"So this is my way of working off some steam!"

Then came the shock wave. Propelled by Kelritch's fist, Fay shot into the air, rocketing over Mahtma's head—straight to the peak of the pyramid.

"Yowch! You actually hit me, didn't you?!"

The god Mahtma II looked up at him. Kelritch crossed her arms; she didn't actually say "Hmph!" but with the look on her face, she might as well have.

Fay turned toward the golden altar, there at the top of the pyramid. "Doesn't matter. Point is, we won this together."

"*I do not deny it*," Mahtma said. The god's form melted away into the sunlight. The deity was satisfied. You could hear it in the last words to resound around the Elements. "*There is no end to the games between humans and the gods. I shall await you, O human, in another game, another time.*"

"Can't wait!" Fay replied.

"*Mm. Therefore, I think it best you keep that flower, until we meet again.*"

The Sun Flower sitting on the altar shone even brighter. Fay shut his eyes tight against the glow...

...and when he opened them again, the god and all the golems were gone, leaving only the desert.

Vs. Mahtma II, the God of the Sun Army—WIN
Game: Sunsteal Scramble
Time Elapsed: 54 minutes, 19 seconds
Win Condition 1: Reach the altar and offer the Sun Flower.
Win Condition 2: Steal the god team's Sun Flower.
Lose Condition: The human team's Sun Flower is stolen.
Rule: Any player who loses their flower(s) after the start of the game is out.

Dropped Item: Sun Flower
Dropped on Difficulty: Mythic
This flower is said to have the power to summon the sun, but exactly what that means is unknown.

# 3

When Fay returned to the real world, he was greeted by a round of applause so thunderous it shook the Dive Center.

"That was spectacular, Fay. You really showed your mettle out there," Chief Secretary Baleggar said. He was in very high spirits. "The stream for this game shattered Mal-ra's viewership record. I knew it was the right choice to invite you here."

"I still have questions, Fay," Kelritch broke in. "If we might continue 'checking our answers'? Dax had the Sun Flower, and he gave it to you moments before he went out. Fair enough. But doesn't that all seem like it would take a lot of good luck?"

"How do you mean?" Fay asked.

"If a person had the Sun Flower, I would have expected them to protect it with their life. But it seems Dax was planning to give you his flower from the beginning."

"Yeah. I think he probably was."

"What's the trick?"

Dax had the Sun Flower—but on the understanding that he would give it to Fay during the game. They couldn't have managed such a complex and important strategy by intuition. Fay and Dax weren't old teammates and comrades in arms; they'd just met a few days ago.

"Don't tell me you were counting on some pie-in-the-sky notion that the two of you would magically just *understand* each other," Kelritch said. "How'd you communicate the plan?"

"During the game, naturally."

"How? Via eye contact?"

"Something a little less subtle than that."

"Kelritch," Dax said, picking up the thread. The black-coated apostle had been listening silently until that moment. "Fay gave me a signal I couldn't miss. And you know it."

"What?"

"Do you remember what he said when the game started?"

"Oh!" Her eyes went wide.

*"I've got the Sun Flower!"* Fay and Leshea had both announced.

And Dax had known what was going on—because *he'd* had the Sun Flower. He knew that Fay and Leshea were both lying.

"The important point is that *only Fay and I* knew that both of their declarations were untrue. That meant a very distinct probability that Fay was sending me a coded message."

Dax had the Sun Flower but Fay had deliberately claimed that *he* had it, in full view of Dax. Kelritch gasped. "If he didn't have it, you simply needed to give it to him!"

"Now you're getting it. I was the only one who could know that's what Fay was really saying."

Fay's announcement hadn't been a message of challenge to the god—it had been a way of communicating the strategy to Dax. And Leshea's announcement? Camouflage, a way of distracting everyone from what Fay was doing.

"To think... Such meaning in such an offhand pronouncement..."

"I'm really sorry I couldn't tell everyone else. Especially you, Pearl," Fay said.

"You *ought* to be sorry!" Pearl said, puffing out her cheeks. "I really gave it my all out there, and just because I thought you'd given me the Sun Flower..."

"It was the only way to throw the god off the scent."

To deceive the gods, first you had to deceive your friends. In fact, Fay's deception had served a purpose. Whether it was Kelritch's fury when Dax went out of the game, or Pearl's fearless charge at Mahtma II—they would have shown none of the same conviction had they known of Fay's plan.

"Anyway, I should be thanking Dax. I needed him to notice what I was doing, and he did," Fay said.

"Child's play. I'd already seen that trick once, after all," Dax replied.

"Huh!" Kelritch said, her eyes going wide again. "Dax...you don't mean in our game of Mind Arena?"

"Precisely. Fay telegraphed his strategy right at the start."

*"I cast the High-Speed spell Encore. It allows me to add one card that's been discarded to the hangar to my hand!"*

He'd planned to use a card—or flower—that had been thrown away to deal the final blow. And Dax had been able to completely comprehend the true meaning of Fay's declaration exactly because he had suffered that loss. And because he hadn't turned away from it, but had carved its lessons into his heart.

"Not that it's of any special interest. I'm not in the business of giving away all my secrets, anyway." Dax flourished his black coat. Only his yellow eyes stayed focused on Fay, which spoke to his superb ability. "Fay! The games that we two eternal rivals shall play have only just begun! I'll be waiting for you on the next field of battle. Let us go, Kelritch!" He turned and left the Dive Center, his footsteps echoing loudly.

"If you'll pardon us, then. Good work today," Kelritch said, and followed him.

Fay watched them for a second, then turned to the dark-haired girl sitting in a corner of the room. She looked like she could hardly contain her excitement. "So," he said, "how do you feel, Nel?"

Nel almost choked. "Wh-whatever do you mean, Master Fay?!" She jumped to her feet. "I mean... You mean... How do *I* feel?"

"You're dripping with sweat," he observed.

This time she blushed. Her fingernails had left marks in her palms, she'd been clenching her fists so hard, and streams of sweat were still soaking her neck. It just went to show how utterly absorbed she had been in the match, how single-mindedly she'd been cheering them on.

And yet...

"Are you really satisfied with this?" Fay asked.

"Wha?!"

"I mean, sure, I'm happy to know you're rooting for us so wholeheartedly. And I'm thrilled that we were able to take the win. But Nel...are you really satisfied? With just being an analyst?"

For a second, she almost didn't breathe. She saw it now. He hadn't given her any choice but to see it: why she was so obsessed with the gods' games even now.

*I never got a team I gelled with, and before I knew it, I was three and out. And when I was at my lowest point, the ideal I found to cling to was...Fay.*

She realized now that she wasn't happy just doing anything as long as she was on his team. She still wanted to be on active duty, playing games. Battling with the gods.

"You're right. I confess... What I really wanted was to try myself in the gods' games alongside you, Master Fay! On the same team!"

"Awesome. Let's do it, then."

"Wha? B-but I lost three times! I had to leave the games..."

On Nel's left hand was a III, the number of defeats she'd suffered

in the gods' games. So long as that marker remained, she wouldn't be able to dive back into any Elements.

Chief Secretary Baleggar broke the silence. "Fay, my friend, you don't mean…," he said, raising his sunglasses. "You can't be about to do what I think you are."

"Sure, I can."

"But…it carries the greatest risk. No one in the entire world has even attempted it in at least twenty years!"

"Believe me, I know." Fay gave the chief secretary a small nod, then turned back to Nel. She gave him a blank look. She wouldn't know, couldn't know, what he and the chief secretary were talking about. It was a secret game, one the Arcane Court had kept hidden for, well, at least twenty years. "Tell me again what your record is, Nel," Fay said.

"My…? Y-you mean, in the gods' games? Three wins, three losses…" Fay didn't say anything immediately. "Master Fay?" Nel asked.

He replied, "I *think* I can make this work." He seemed to be speaking to himself—then he glanced at the chief secretary. "I know it's sudden, Chief Secretary Baleggar, but could you get in touch with Chief Secretary Miranda for me? Tell her we're going to face the Bookmaker."

# Player.7
## The Retiree Who Wouldn't Give Up

Rule six of the seven covenants of the gods' games: apostles who lose three games in total are disqualified from further participation.

It had been thus since antiquity. But if there was one thing humanity had learned from the games, it was that the gods had their whims. There was a saying in the human world: what one god abandons, another might pick up. Just so, once in a blue moon there could be found among the countless deities some strange character who would deign to play with a retired apostle.

"A contest where you wager for a 'retry'? You're right, it's been done before."

They were in a twelfth-floor guest room of the Mal-ra Arcane Court branch office, in front of a screen on which Chief Secretary Miranda could be seen sighing. She thought they might be getting in over their heads, as her tone of voice made clear. "The gods love games, so they wouldn't abandon someone who sincerely won't give up the challenge. I'm impressed you remembered, Fay."

"Only vaguely. That's why I wanted to double-check with you, Chief Secretary."

"Well, you're right. There's a god called the Bookmaker, who will play with you if you wager one of your wins. You would bet one of your victories, Fay, and if you won, one of Nel's losses would be erased."

With ordinary gods, you were granted one win if you defeated them and one loss if they defeated you. With the Bookmaker, if you were victorious, one loss would be undone, while if you were defeated, one of your wins would be taken away.

Most gods had the power to increase the number of an apostle's wins or losses—but the Bookmaker had the power to reduce them.

"You can only reach the Bookmaker from one particular kind of Divine Gate. Which I guess makes sense for such a...unique god. But Mal-ra doesn't have one. It's not surprising you would never have heard about this, Nel." There were no records at the Arcane Court of anyone taking on the Bookmaker in more than thirty years, and Mal-ra didn't even have one of the Divine Gates necessary to reach them. It was hard to blame Nel for not knowing about it.

"But we have one, don't we?" Fay said. "In Ruin?"

"If you must know... Yes." On the screen, Miranda sighed again.

*"If you'd be so kind as to have a look at this, Lady Leshea. The Dive Request status of the Divine Gates in the branch office's possession. We have five in total, although as one of them is currently out of use, only four are available."*

\*          \*          \*

One of Ruin's Gates was unused—the one that led to the Bookmaker.

"It's been... Gosh, almost forty years for us, I guess. That Gate is probably buried in dust by now. Oh! Uh, that's just a figure of speech. I assure you we keep it clean and in working order."

Fay was holding a piece of paper: a printout of the data Miranda had sent him first thing that morning.

A match with the Bookmaker worked like this:

1. A human played a one-on-one against the Bookmaker.

2. The bet was one victory belonging to a compatriot. In this case, Fay would furnish the "coin."

3. If the challenger—Nel—won, one of her losses would be expunged, meaning she would go from a 3-3 record to 3-2.

4. If Nel lost, Fay would lose the win he'd wagered, going from 6-0 to 5-0.

"I see. So it's Nel who would challenge the Bookmaker, using my victory. If she wins, one of her losses would go away, taking her down to two—which would give her room to become an active apostle again."

"Y-you can't! You can't *do* that!" cried none other than Nel herself. She clenched her fists and gave him a terrible look. "If I lost, you'd lose a victory! That's much too important to wager!"

"Naw, it's fine."

"H-how can you *say* that, Master Fay?!"

Fay's record in the gods' games was 6-0, already a streak practically unheard of in human history. A true record if there ever was one. There was every chance he would come up against still stronger gods in the future, deities who might pose a real threat to his progress, but at this rate ten wins didn't feel like a fantasy. The possibility of a Clear, the first in human history, seemed within reach.

"Can you imagine if a total stranger like me wagered one of your six wins and *lost* it, Master Fay?" Nel said.

"It would be a treasure slipping through humanity's fingers, that's for sure," Miranda agreed. She rested her chin on her hands and went on quietly, "Speaking as a chief secretary of the Arcane Court, Fay's wins are the literal hope of humanity. To risk one of them on behalf of someone who could only manage three victories would be absurd. As I think you understand, right, Nel?"

Nel's response was a strained silence.

"I realize you wouldn't necessarily guess from looking at Fay's record, but achieving even one victory in the gods' games is extraordinarily difficult. Just to put it in perspective, I've gotten reports from three different games today, and all of them were losses."

The average winning ratio across all the gods' games was eleven percent. The fact was that behind the handful of consistent winners like Fay and the Dragon God Leoleshea, there were hundreds and hundreds of apostles suffering abject defeats.

"You'd be risking a victory that humanity fought tooth and nail to get. Statistically, a fair wager for one victory wouldn't be one loss—it'd be more like ten. But even if you beat the Bookmaker, we only get back one loss. That's not commensurate. It's practically a swindle."

The wager didn't make statistical sense, not if a victory was worth ten times more than a loss. Yet the Bookmaker would expect them to treat a win and a loss as equal in the scales of this game.

"That's why nobody goes to this Bookmaker anymore. It's why you've never heard of them. The Bookmaker hasn't even been part of the conversation for decades!" Miranda let out a long, dramatic sigh. "Tell me something, Nel. How badly do you want to make this comeback? Badly enough to risk pissing away one of Fay's victories?"

Nel caught her breath.

"Do you know how many apostles have had to withdraw from the Arcane Court over the course of history? Plenty of them were heroes, people with six or even seven wins." But heroes followed the same rules as everyone else. Three losses, and they had to leave the games. "And now you, with only three victories to your name, are going to bet one of Fay's wins just because you want to join him and Lady Leshea on the world's greatest team?"

"W-well... I..."

"I know it sounds awful to put it this way—but are you sure you're worth that much?"

The dark-haired girl sucked in a breath and bit her lip. She looked at the ground, her shoulders slumping.

It was at that moment that Pearl spoke up. "Th-then she can wager one of my victories! I agree completely that Fay's wins are too important. But... But she could have one of mine. To bet with. That would solve our problem!"

"Pearl?!" Nel turned toward her like a shot. On-screen, Miranda was speechless.

"Nel... I know you cheered yourself hoarse rooting for us," Pearl said.

"Aww, is kinship doing its work?" Miranda said. Her gaze was hard, but Pearl looked right back at her and placed her hand on her chest.

"I—I know people say I'm quick to jump to conclusions! But I know that Nel is so eager to play games with us. I can tell!"

"Well, there you have it, Chief Secretary," Fay said, putting a hand on Pearl's back and taking a step forward. "You heard the lady. But I think she should go ahead and wager one of my victories."

He meant it. There was a reason he wanted it to be his win on the line, and no one else's.

"That cool with you, Leshea?" Fay asked.

"Hmm. I'd be perfectly happy to offer one of mine." Leshea sounded completely unbothered—and looked toward the screen, too; she was sitting on a sofa in the middle of the room, playing a game of Go against herself. "Say, Miranda?" she said.

"Yes, Lady Leoleshea?"

"Speaking as a former deity myself, I can tell you that the gods really couldn't care less about apostles who wish they could make a comeback. Humans who go around telling everyone they *wish* they could try again, praying for it? Not interested. The gods only smile on those who make their own miracles."

And Nel had done just that. She'd screwed up her courage to talk to them, thrown away her pride to beg them for help, and had struggled alongside them. Her miracle hadn't come yet...but she'd done everything she needed to do to make it happen.

"I don't know how many retired apostles there are, thousands or tens of thousands or whatever, but only one of them went out of their way to do all that for me and Fay—it was Nel. I think that makes her worth a look."

"I can't disagree with you there," Miranda said after a second.

"Well, I guess that settles it!" Leshea chirped.

"You realize this is a serious team, not a social club, right?" Miranda said, but she knew she was beaten. It was easy to tell from the small smile that crept across her face as she looked up at the ceiling. "All right, I'll get things in order. You'll be able to challenge the Bookmaker as soon as you get back."

"Well, then," Fay said with a small sigh. He turned and nodded at Nel; her face was a mask of tension. "Nothing's happened yet. All we can do is get the miraculous pins lined up. And you'll do it, right? You're gonna make that comeback."

For a long moment, Nel didn't say anything.

"Go out there and win this one."

"I will! I absolutely will!" Nel's eyes were shining. "Thank you, Master Fay! Lady Leoleshea! And you, Pearl! I can't thank any of you enough. You especially, Master Fay! I have no idea how I'm going to repay this debt!"

"Like I said, no worries about betting my wins. If it takes you a couple of tries, just keep—"

"Absolutely not!" Nel shook her head. "I'll borrow one win from you, Master Fay. And I'll give it back just like I found it. I'm going to beat the Bookmaker—just watch me!"

They'd only have about a week to wait...

# Epilogue
## The Bookmaker

They were in a modest subspace, the smallest Elements Fay had encountered—but the god described it as the field of play.

"*Sigh...*" The voice echoing around the subspace wasn't that of a human. It was a god's disappointed exhalation. "*Boring. Pathetic, even. You got steamrolled, human.*"

The response was a very, very long silence. The only furnishing in this Elements was a single poker table. Facing each other across it were two young women with dark hair.

*Two Nel Recklesses.*

One of them wore a condescending smile, her recently revealed trump card on the table. The other was slumped to her knees on the ground.

"I can't... I can't believe this..."

"*There were no divine tweaks to this game. I challenged you to a round of perfectly ordinary human poker. I thrashed you once, made you cry the second time, and crushed you the third. You've lost every hand.*"

Nel looked down at Nel. But the two of them weren't quite identical: where the real Nel had eyes the color of amethyst, her double's were amber. A small detail that gave away the deception.

\*     \*     \*

Gremoire, the Polymorphic God.

This was a god of no one form and many names: Mimic, Shapeshifter, Doppelgänger, and more besides. Including the Bookmaker. By the time Nel had arrived in Gremoire's Elements, the god was already waiting for her in her own form.

*"A human challenger after so long... I hoped for better."*

Nel had no response.

*"I know what you were thinking. It was blindingly obvious. You were betting with your precious friend's victories, so you absolutely, positively couldn't let yourself lose. You couldn't make any risky bets."*

The god in Nel's form threw down its cards—all five of them were trumps. They drifted through the air and settled on the floor in front of the broken Nel, mocking her.

*"You'll never undo this girl's losses."* The Bookmaker turned away from the downtrodden Nel, all interest in her gone. Instead, the deity turned to Fay. *"And of course, I'll claim those three victories I've got coming to me. The ones you wagered."*

Fay didn't say anything, but he felt a dull pain in his right hand. The VI that had been carved there, the mark of the gods, disappeared, replaced by a III.

Fay's record in the gods' games went from 6-0 to 3-0.

He stood in silence. Nel was so shattered that she couldn't even speak. Pearl watched the entire thing blankly, and Leshea had to fight to hold her tongue. The Bookmaker shot the four visitors a look. *"Talk about boring. What a letdown."* The god sighed just like a human would, a sound of genuine disappointment. Not with Nel the human—but with its own thwarted hopes. This was a god who hadn't had a chance to play a game in decades, and the pleasure of the opportunity had been denied it. Simple, childish—or was that godly?—frustration. *"Here I thought I might be able to enjoy a game for once. Go home, humans."*

Bookmaker Nel turned its back on them.

"Just a second," Fay said. The Bookmaker was walking away. "This is where the game really starts, and you know it."

That stopped the Bookmaker in its tracks. *"Oh, I do, do I? What exactly do you mean, human?"*

"I mean everything's going exactly the way I planned."

*"Hrm?"*

"Bookmaker," Fay said, staring straight at the Polymorphic God in Nel's body, "I win this game."

*"You...what?"*

"From the moment you accepted this match, I knew I'd be victorious. No matter how things turned out. And it's all gone exactly the way I expected." Fay wasn't challenging the god—he was going straight to declaring victory. "I told you, right, Nel? It'd be great if you won, but you didn't have to feel down if you lost?"

"Wha...?"

"All right, switch off with me." Nel was still staring at Fay in befuddlement as he patted her on the shoulder and gave her a bracing smile. "Looks like this isn't quite making sense to you. That's fine. I'll be happy to explain everything soon. But first..."

He looked the Bookmaker in its amber eyes.

"Now it's my turn to play. *Then* we can check our answers."

# Afterword

*"Fay! I was right— you and I are destined to be rivals all our lives!"*

Welcome to *Gods' Games We Play*, Volume 2, and thank you for your patience! Normally this series revolves around the games people play against the all-powerful, all-knowing gods, but in this volume, we've got some human-versus-human action, a sort of athletic competition, to spice things up. I hope you'll continue to enjoy this story of a world where humans and gods are equally mad about games!

And speaking of games...

Sometimes your own author gets excited about these ideas, like, what if we had a game like this in the real world?! In this volume, I think Mind Arena is like that: a game where your play options are virtually unlimited based on your combination of cards and class. Maybe we'll see something like that in the real world someday...is what I was thinking the whole time I was writing Volume 2! (Ahem... I have a design doc if anyone would like to see it...haha...)

Nel and Fay seem to be in dire straits in the epilogue of this volume, so how can Fay declare victory? I hope you'll join us in Volume 3 to find out!

Notice of *Our Last Crusade* crossover!
You might be aware of another series by yours truly, *Our Last*

*Crusade or the Rise of a New World.* (It even had an anime in 2020!) Volume 11 came out on May 20 of 2021. In honor of that book and *Gods' Games We Play* Volume 2 being published in the same month, readers who purchase both books can receive a special short story.

As ever, this book wouldn't exist without a lot of help. That includes my editor K, who went through the whole process with me, and Toiro Tomose, who created another batch of god-tier illustrations for this volume. I'd also like to take this opportunity to thank konomi and GreeN, who took time out of their busy schedules to do celebratory illustrations for the series!

And of course, to all of you who have picked up this book, thank you so much! I expect Volume 3 to come out around early autumn. Can Fay outwit a god who doesn't play by the rules?! Tune in and find out!

Kei Sazane
*A spring noon*